# A Master's Degree

## Margaret Hill McCarter

TO THE KANSAS BOYS AND GIRLS
WHO HAVE NOT YET EARNED THEIR DEGREES;
AND TO THOSE OLDER IN YEARS, EVERYWHERE,
"CAPTAINS OVER HUNDREDS,"
WHO WOULD WIN TO THE LARGER MASTERY.

In the old days there were angels who came and took men by the hand and led them away from the city of destruction. We see no white-winged angels now. But yet men are led away from threatening destruction: a hand is put into theirs, which leads them gently forth toward a calm and bright land, so that they look no more backward; and the hand may be a little child's.

GEORGE ELIOT

# CONTENTS

# THE MEETING

...There is neither East nor West, Border, nor Breed, nor Birth,
When two strong men stand face to face, tho' they come from the
ends of the earth!
KIPLING

IT happened by mere chance that the September day on which Professor Vincent Burgess, A.B., from Boston, first entered Sunrise College as instructor in Greek, was the same day on which Vic Burleigh, overgrown country boy from a Kansas claim out beyond the Walnut River, signed up with the secretary of the College Board and paid the entrance fee for his freshman year. And further, by chance, it happened that the two young men had first met at the gateway to the campus, one coming from the East and the other from the West, and having exchanged the courtesies of stranger greeting, they had walked, side by side, up the long avenue to the foot of the slope. Together, they had climbed the broad flight of steps leading up to the imposing doorway of Sunrise, with the great letter S carved in stone relief above it; and, after pausing a moment to take in the matchless wonder of the landscape over which old Sunrise keeps watch, the college portal had swung open, and the two had entered at the same time.

Inside the doorway the Professor and the country boy were impressed, though in differing degrees, with the massive beauty of the rotunda over which the stained glass of the dome hangs a halo of mellow radiance. Involuntarily they lifted their eyes toward this crown of light and saw far above them, wrought in dainty coloring, the design of the great State Seal of Kansas, with its inscription They saw something more in that upward glance. On the stairway of the rotunda, Elinor Wream, the niece of the president of Sunrise College, was leaning over the balustrade, looking at them with curious eyes. Her smile of recognition as she caught sight of Professor Burgess, gave place to an expression of half-concealed ridicule, as she glanced down at Vic Burleigh, the big, heavy-boned young fellow, so grotesquely impossible to the harmony of the place.

As the two men dropped their eyes, they encountered the upturned face of a plainly dressed girl coming up the stairs from the basement, with a big feather duster in her hand. It was old Bond Saxon's daughter Dennie, who was earning her tuition by keeping the library and offices in order. As if to even matters, it was Vic Burleigh who caught a token of recognition now, while the young Professor was surveyed with fearless disapproval.

All this took only a moment of time. Long afterward these two men knew that in that moment an antagonism was born between them that must fight itself out through the length of days. But now, Dr. Lloyd Fenneben, Dean of Sunrise, known to students and alumni alike as "Dean Funnybone," was grasping each man's hand with a cordial grip and measuring each with a keen glance from piercing black eyes, as he bade them equal welcome.

And here all likeness of conditions ends for these two. Days come and go, moons wax and wane, seedtime and harvest, cold and heat, summer and winter glide fourfold through their appointed seasons, before the two young men stand side by side on a common level again. And the events of these changing seasons ring in so rapidly, and in so inevitable a fashion, that the whole cycle runs like a real story along the page.

### STRIFE

With the first faint note out of distance flung,
   From the moment man hears the siren call
   Of Victory's bugle, which sounds for all,
   To his inner self the promise is made
   To weary not, rest not, but all unafraid
Press on—till for him the paean be sung.

The song for the victor is sweet, is sweet—
   Yet to the music a memory clings
   Of trampled nestlings, of broken wings,
And of faces white with defeat!
        —ELIZABETH D. PRESTON

## CHAPTER I. "DEAN FUNNYBONE"

Nature they say, doth dote,
And cannot make a man
Save on some worn-out plan,
Repeating us by rote:
For him her Old-World moulds aside she threw,

.............................

With stuff untainted,
shaped a hero new. —LOWELL

DR. LLOYD FENNEBEN, Dean of Sunrise College, had migrated to the Walnut Valley with the founding of the school here. In fact, he had brought the college with him when he came hither, and had set it, as a light not to be hidden, on the crest of that high ridge that runs east of the little town of Lagonda Ledge. And the town eagerly took the new school to itself; at once its pride and profit. Yea, the town rises and sets with Sunrise. When the first gleam of morning, hidden by the east ridge from the Walnut Valley, glints redly from the south windows of the college dome in the winter time, and from the north windows in the summer time, the town bestirs; itself, and the factory whistles blow. And when the last crimson glory of evening puts a halo of flame about the brow of Sunrise, the people know that out beyond the Walnut River the day is passing, and the pearl-gray mantle of twilight is deepening to velvety darkness on the wide, quiet prairie lands.

Lagonda Ledge was a better place after the college settled permanently above it. Some improvident citizens took a new hold on life, while some undesirables who had lived in lawless infamy skulked across the Walnut and disappeared in that rough picturesque region full of uncertainties that lies behind the west bluffs of the stream. All this, after the college had found an abiding place on the limestone ridge. For Sunrise had been a migratory bird before reaching the outskirts of Lagonda Ledge. As a fulfillment of prophecy, it had arisen from the visions and pockets of some Boston scholars, and it had come to the West and was made flesh —or stone—and dwelt among men on the outskirts of a booming young Kansas town.

Lloyd Fenneben was just out of Harvard when Dr. Joshua Wream, his step-brother, many years his senior, professor of all the dead languages ever left unburied, had put a considerable fortune into his hands, and into his brain the dream of a life-work—even the building of a great university in the West. For the Wreams were a stubborn, self-willed, bookish breed, who held that salvation of souls could come only through possession of a college diploma. Young Fenneben had come to Kansas with all his youth and health and money, with high ideals and culture and ambition for success and dreams of honor—and, hidden deep down, the memory of some sort of love affair, but that was his own business. With this dream of a new Harvard on the western prairies, he had burned his bridges behind him, and in an unbusiness-like way, relying too much upon a board of trustees whom he had interested in his plans he had eagerly begun his task, struggling to adapt the West to his university model, measuring all men and means by the scholarly rule of his Alma Mater. Being a young man, he took himself full seriously, and it was a tremendous blow to his sense of dignity when the youthful Jayhawkers at the outset dubbed him "Dean Funnybone"—a name he was never to lose.

His college flourished so amazingly that another boom town, farther inland, came across the prairie one day, and before the eyes of the young dean bought it of the money-loving trustees—body and soul and dean—and packed it off as the Plains Indians would carry off a white captive, miles away to the westward. Plumped down in a big frame barracks in the public square of twenty acres in the middle of this new town, at once real estate dealers advertised the place as the literary center of Kansas; while lots in straggling additions far away across the prairie draws were boomed as "college flats within walking distance of the university."

In this new setting Lloyd Fenneben started again to build up what had been so recklessly torn down. But it was slow doing, and in a downcast hour the head of the board of trustees took council with the young dean.

"Funnybone, that's what the boys call you, ain't it?" The name had come along over the prairie with the school. "Funnybone, you are as likely a man as ever escaped from Boston. But you're never going to build the East into the West, no more'n you could ram the West into the Atlantic seaboard states. My advice to you is to get yourself into the West for good and drop your higher learnin' notions, and be one of us, or beat it back to where you came from quick."

Dean Fenneben listened as a man who hears the reading of his own obituary.

"You've come out to Kansas with beautiful dreams," the bluff trustee continued. "Drop 'em! You're too late for the New England pioneers who come West. They've had their day and passed on. The thing for you to do is to commercialize yourself right away. Go to buyin' and sellin' dirt. It's all a man can do for Kansas now. Just boom her real estate."

"All a man can do for Kansas!" Fenneben repeated slowly.

"Sure, and I'll tell you something more. This town is busted, absolutely busted. I, and a few others, brought this college here as an investment for ourselves. It ain't paid us, and we've throwed the thing over. I've just closed a deal with a New Jersey syndicate that gets me rid of every foot of ground I own here. The county-seat's goin' to be eighteen miles south, and it will be kingdom come, a'most, before the railroad extension is any nearer 'n that. Let your university go, and come with me. I can make you rich in six months. In six weeks the coyotes will be howlin' through your college halls, and the prairie dogs layin' out a townsite on the campus, and the rattlesnakes coilin' round the doorsteps. Will you come, Funnybone?"

The trustee waited for an answer. While he waited, the soul of the young dean found itself.

"Funnybone!" Lloyd repeated. "I guess that's just what I need—a funny bone in my anatomy to help me to see the humor of this thing. Go with you and give up my college? Build up the prosperity of a commonwealth by starving its mind! No, no; I'll go on with the thing I came here to do—so help me God!"

"You'll soon go to the devil, you and your old school. Good-by!" And the trustee left him.

A month later, Dean Fenneben sat alone in his university barracks and saw the prairie dogs making the dust fly as they digged about what had been intended for a flower bed on the campus. Then he packed up his meager library and other college equipments and walked ten miles across the plains to hire a man with a team to haul them away. The teamster had much ado to drive his half-bridle-wise Indian ponies near enough to the university doorway to load his wagon. Before the threshold a huge rattlesnake lay coiled, already disputing any human claim to this kingdom of the wild.

Discouraging as all this must have been to Fenneben, when he started away from the deserted town he smiled joyously as a man who sees his road fair before him.

"I might go back to Cambridge and poke about after the dead languages until my brother passes on, and then drop into his chair in the university," he said to himself, "but the trustee was right. I can never build the East into the West. But I can learn from the East how to bring the West into its own kingdom. I can make the dead languages serve me the better to speak the living words here. And if I can do that, I may earn a Master's Degree from my Alma Mater without the writing of a learned thesis to clinch it. But whether I win honor or I am forgotten, this shall be my life-work—out on these Kansas prairies, to till a soil that shall grow MEN AND WOMEN."

For the next three years Dean Fenneben and his college flourished on the borders of a little frontier town, if that can be called flourishing which uses up time, and money, and energy, Christian patience, and dogged persistence. Then an August prairie fire, sweeping up from the southwest, leaped the narrow fire-guard about the one building and burned up everything there, except Dean Fenneben. Six years, and nothing to show for his work on the outside. Inside, the six years' stay in Kansas had seen the making over of a scholarly dreamer into a hard-headed, far-seeing, masterful man, who took the

West as he found it, but did not leave it so. Not he! All the power of higher learning he still held supreme. But by days of hard work in the college halls, and nights of meditation out in the silent sanctuary spaces of the prairies round about him, he had been learning how to compute the needs of men as the angel with the golden reed computed the walls and gates of the New Jerusalem — *according to the measure of a man.*

Such was Dean Fenneben who came after six years of service to the little town of Lagonda Ledge to plant Sunrise on the crest above the Walnut Valley beyond reach of prairie fire or bursting boom. Firm set as the limestone of its foundations, he reared here a college that should live, for that its builder himself with his feet on the ground and his face toward the light had learned the secret of living.

Miles away across the valley, the dome of Sunrise could be seen by day. By night, the old college lantern at first, and later the studding of electric lights, made a beacon for all the open countryside. But if the wayfarer, by chance or choice, turned his footsteps to those rocky bluffs and glens beyond the Walnut River, wherefrom the town of Lagonda Ledge takes its name, he lost the guiding ray from the hilltop and groped in black and dangerous ways where darkness rules.

Above the south turret hung the Sunrise bell, whose resonant voice filled the whole valley, and what the sight of Sunrise failed to do for Lagonda Ledge, the sound of the bell accomplished. The first class to enter the school nicknamed its head "Dean Funnybone," but this gave him no shock any more. He had learned the humor of life now, the spirit of the open land where the view is broad to broadening souls.

And it was to the hand of Dean Fenneben that Professor Vincent Burgess, A.B., Greek instructor from Boston, and Vic Burleigh, the big country boy from a claim beyond the Walnut, came on a September day; albeit, the one had his head in the clouds, while the other's feet were clogged with the grass roots.

## CHAPTER II. POTTER'S CLAY

This clay, well mixed with marl and sand,
Follows the motion of my hand,
For some must follow and some command,
  Though all are made of clay.
    —LONGFELLOW

THE afternoon sunshine was flooding the September landscape with molten gold, filling the valley with intense heat, and rippling back in warm waves from the crest of the ridge. Dean Fenneben's study in the south tower of Sunrise looked out on the new heaven and the new earth, every day-dawn created afresh for his eyes; for truly, the Walnut Valley in any mood needs only eyes that see to be called a goodly land. And it was because of the magnificent vista, unfolding in woodland, and winding river, and fertile field, and far golden prairie—it was because of the unconscious power of all this upon the student mind, that Dr. Fenneben had set his college up here.

On this September afternoon, the Dean sat looking out on this land of pure delight a-quiver in the late summer sunshine. Nature had done well by Lloyd Fenneben. His height was commanding, and he was slender, rather than heavy, with ease of movement as if the play of every muscle was nerved to harmony. His heavy black hair was worn a trifle long on the upper part of his head and fell in masses above his forehead. His eyes were black and keen under heavy black brows. Every feature was strong and massive, but saved from sternness by a genial kindliness and sense of humor. Whoever came into his presence felt that magnetic power only a king of his kind can possess.

Long the Dean sat gazing at the gleaming landscape and the sleepy town beyond the campus and the pigeons circling gracefully above a little cottage, hidden by trees, up the river.

"A wonderful region!" he murmured. "If that old white-haired brother of mine digging about the roots of Greek and Sanscrit back in Harvard could only see all this, maybe he might understand why I choose to stay here with my college instead of tying up with a university back East. But, maybe not. We are only step-brothers. He is old enough to be my father, and with all his knowledge of books he could never read men. However, he sent me West with a fat pocketbook in the interest of higher education. I hope I've invested well. And our magnificent group of buildings up here and our broad-acred campus, together with our splendid enrollment of students justify my hope. Strange, I have never known whose money I was using. Not Joshua Wream's, I know that. Money is nothing to the Wreams except as it endows libraries, builds colleges, and extends universities. Too scholarly for these prairies, all of them! Too scholarly!"

The Dean's eyes were fixed on a tiny shaft of blue smoke rising steadily from the rough country in the valley beyond Lagonda Ledge, but his mind was still on his brother.

"Dr. Joshua Wream, D.D., Litt.D., LL.D., etc.! He has taken all the degrees conferable, except the degree of human insight." Something behind the strong face sent a line of pathos into it with the thought. "He has piled up enough for me to look after this fall, anyhow. It was bad enough for that niece of ours to be left a penniless orphan with only the two uncles to look after her and both of us bachelors. And now, after he has been shaping Elinor Wream's life until she is ready for college, he sends her out here to me, frankly declaring that she is too much for him. She always was."

He turned to a letter lying on the table beside him, a smile playing about the frown on his countenance.

"He hopes I can do better by Elinor than he has been able to do, because he's never had a wife nor child to teach him," he continued, giving word to his thought. "A fine time for me to begin! No wife nor child has ever taught me anything. He says she is a good girl, a beautiful girl with only two great faults. Only two! She's lucky. 'One'"—Fenneben glanced more closely at the letter—"'is her self-will.' I never knew a Wream that didn't have that fault. 'And the other'"—the frown drove back the smile now—"'is her notion of wealth. Nobody but a rich man could ever win her hand.' She who has been simply reared, with all the Wream creed that higher education is the final end of man, is set with a Wream-like firmness

9

in her hatred of poverty, her eagerness for riches and luxury. And to add to all this responsibility he must send me his pet Greek scholar, Vincent Burgess, to try out as a professor in Sunrise. A Burgess, of all men in the world, to be sent to me! Of course this young man knows nothing of my affairs but is my brother too old and too scholarly to remember what I've tried a thousand times to forget? I thought the old wound had healed by this time."

A wave of sadness swept the strong man's face. "I've asked Burgess to come up at three. I must find out what material is sent here for my shaping. It is a president's business to shape well, and I must do my best, God help me!"

A shadow darkened Lloyd Fenneben's face, and his black eyes held a strange light. He stared vacantly at the landscape until he suddenly noted the slender wavering pillar of smoke beyond the Walnut.

"There are no houses in those glens and hidden places," he thought. "I wonder what fire is under that smoke on a day like this. It is a far cry from the top of this ridge to the bottom of that half-tamed region down there. One may see into three counties here, but it is rough traveling across the river by day, and worse by night."

The bell above the south turret chimed the hour of three as Vincent Burgess entered the study.

"Take this seat by the window," Dr. Fenneben said with a genial smile and a handclasp worth remembering. "You can see an Empire from this point, if you care to look out."

Vincent Burgess sat at ease in any presence. He had the face of a scholar, and the manners of a gentleman. But he gave no sign that he cared to view the empire that lay beyond the window.

"We are to be co-workers for some time, Burgess. May I ask you why you chose to come to Kansas?"

Fenneben came straight to the purpose of the interview. This keen-eyed, business-like man seemed to Burgess very unlike old Dr. Wream, whom everybody at Harvard loved and anybody could deceive. But to the direct question he answered directly and concisely.

"I came to study types, to acquire geographical breadth, to have seclusion, that I may pursue more profound research."

There was a play of light in Dr. Fenneben's eyes.

"You must judge for yourself of the value of Sunrise and Lagonda Ledge for seclusion. But we make a specialty of geographical breadth out here. As to types, they assay fairly well to the ton, these Jayhawkers do."

"What are Jayhawkers, Doctor?" Burgess queried.

"Yonder is one specimen," Fenneben answered, pointing toward the window.

Vincent Burgess, looking out, saw Vic Burleigh leaping up the broad steps from the level campus, a giant fellow, fully six feet tall. The swing of strength, void of grace, was in his motion. His face was gypsy-brown under a crop of sunburned auburn hair. A stiff new derby hat was set bashfully on a head set unabashed on broad shoulders. The store-mark of the ready-made was on his clothing, and it was clear that he was less accustomed to cut stone steps than to springing prairie sod. Clearly he was a real product of the soil.

"Why, that is the young bumpkin I came in with this morning. I thought I was striding alongside an elephant in bulk and wild horse in speed," Burgess said with a smile.

"You will have a share in taming him, doubtless," Dr. Fenneben replied. "He looks hardly bridle-wise yet. Enter him among your types. I didn't get his name this morning, but he interested me at once, as a fellow of good blood if not of good manners, and I have asked him to come in here later. Some boys must be met on the very threshold of a college if they are to run safely along the four years."

"His name is Burleigh, Victor Burleigh. I remember it because it is not a new name to me. Picture him in a cap and gown at home in a library, or standing up to receive a Master's Degree from a university! His kind leave about the middle of the second semester and revert to the soil, don't they?"

Burgess laughed pleasantly, and leaned forward to get one more look at the country boy, disappearing behind a group of evergreens in the north angle of the building.

"They do not always leave so soon as that. You can't tell the grade of timber every time by the bark outside." There was a deeper tone in Dr. Fenneben's voice now. "But as to yourself, you had a motive in coming to Kansas, I judge. You can study types anywhere."

Whether the young man liked this or not, he answered evenly:

"I am to give instruction in Greek here at Lagonda Ledge. Beastly name, isn't it? Suggestive of rattlesnakes, somehow! I shall spend much time in study, for I am preparing a comprehensive thesis for my Master's Degree. The very barrenness of these dull prairies will keep me close to my library for a couple of years."

"Oh, you will do your work well anywhere," Dr. Fenneben declared. "You need not put walls of distances about you for that. I thought you might have a more definite purpose in choosing this state, of all places."

Fenneben's mind was running back to the days of his own first struggle for existence in the West, and his heart went out in sympathy to the undisciplined young professor.

"I have a reason, but it is entirely a personal matter." Burgess was looking at the floor now. "Did you know I had a sister once?"

"Yes, I know," Dr. Fenneben said.

"She was married and came to Kansas. That was after you left Cambridge, I suppose. She and her husband are both dead, leaving no children. My father was bitterly opposed to her coming out here, and never forgave her for it. He died recently, making me his heir. I've always thought I'd like to see the state where my sister lived. She died young. She could not have been as old as you are, and you are a young man yet, Doctor. In addition, my father left in my care some trust funds for a claimant who also lived in Kansas. He is dead now, but I want to find out something more definite concerning him. Outside of this, I hope to do well here and to succeed to higher places elsewhere, soon. All this personal to myself, and worthy, I hope."

He looked at Fenneben, who was leaning forward with his elbow on the table and his head bowed. His face was hidden and his white fingers were thrust through the heavy masses of black hair.

"You will find a great field here in which to work out your success," the Dean said at length. "But I must give a word of warning. I tried once to reproduce the eastern university here. I learned better. If Kansas is to be your training ground, may I say that the man who opens his front door for the first time on the green prairies of the West has no less to learn than the man who first pitches his tent beside the blue Atlantic? Don't say I didn't show you where to find the blazed trail if you get lost from it for a little while."

Dr. Fenneben's face was charming when he smiled.

"One other thing I may mention. You know my niece, Elinor? I've been out here so long, I may need your help in making her feel at home at first."

There was a new light in Burgess's eyes at the mention of Elinor Wream's name.

"Oh, yes, I know Miss Elinor very well. I shall need her more to make me feel at home than she will need me."

Somehow the answer was a trifle too quick and smooth to ring right. Dr. Fenneben forgot it in an instant, however, for Elinor Wream herself came suddenly into the room, a tall, slender girl, with a face so full of sunshiny charm that no great defect of character had yet made its mark there.

"I beg your pardon, Uncle Lloyd; I thought you were alone. How do you do, Professor Burgess." She came forward smilingly and offered her hand. "Makes me homesick for old Cambridge and Uncle Joshua when I see you. I want to go down to Lagonda Ledge, and I don't know the streets at all. Don't you want to show me the way?"

"Can't you wait for me to do that, Norrie? I have only one more engagement for the afternoon, and Miss Saxon will be wanting to dust in here soon." Dr. Fenneben looked fondly at his niece, a man to make other men jealous, if occasion offered.

"Please don't, Miss Elinor," Vincent Burgess urged. "I shall be delighted to explore darkest Kansas with you at any time."

"There is no mistaking that look in a man's eyes," Dr. Fenneben thought as he watched the two pass through the rotunda and out of the great front door. "I have guessed Joshua's plan easily enough, but I've only half guessed him out. Why did he mention his money matters to me? There is enough merit in him worth the shaping Sunrise will give him, however, and I must do a man's part, anyhow. As for Elinor, there's a ready-made missionary field in her, so Joshua warns me. But he is a poor judge sometimes. I wish I might have begun with her sooner. I cannot think she is quite as mercenary as he represents her to be."

Through the window he saw a pretty picture. Outlined against the dark green cedars of the north angle was Professor Burgess, tall, slender, fair of face, faultless in dress. Beside him was Elinor Wream, all dainty and sweet and white, from the broad-brimmed hat set jauntily on her dark hair to the white bows on the instep of her neat little canvas shoes. A wave of loneliness swept over Dr. Fenneben's soul as he looked.

"It must have been a thousand years ago that I was in love and walked in my Eden. There are no serpents here as there were in mine."

Just then his eyes fell upon the wide stone landing of the campus steps. At the same moment Elinor gave a scream of fright. A bull snake, big and ugly, had crawled half out of the burned grasses of the slope and stretched itself lazily in the sunshine along the warm stone. It roused itself at the scream, emitting its hoarse hiss, after the manner of bull snakes. Elinor clutched at her companion's arm, pale with fear.

"Kill it! Kill it!" she cried, trying to force her slender white parasol into his hand.

Before he could move, Vic Burleigh leaped out from behind the cedars, and, picking up a sharp-edged bit of limestone, tipped his hand dexterously and sent it clean as a knife cut across the space. It struck the snake just below the head, half severing it from the body. Another leap and Burleigh had kicked the whole writhing mass—it would have measured five feet—off the stone into the sunflower stalks and long grasses of the steep slope.

"How did you ever dare?" Elinor asked.

"Oh, he's not poison; he just doesn't belong up here."

The bluntness of timidity was in Vic's answer, but the strength and musical depth of his resonant voice was almost startling.

"There is no Eden without a serpent, Miss Elinor," Professor Burgess said lightly.

"Nor a serpent without some sort of Eden built around it. The thing's mate will be along after it pretty soon. Look out for it down there. The best place to catch it is right behind its ears," came the boy's quick response.

Burleigh looked back defiantly at Burgess as he disappeared indoors. And the antagonism born in the meeting of these two men in the morning took on a tiny degree of strength in the afternoon.

"What a wonderful voice, Vincent. It makes one want to hear it again," Elinor exclaimed.

"Yes, and what an overgrown pile of awkwardness. It makes one hope never to see it again," her companion responded.

"But he killed that snake in a way that looked expert to me," Elinor insisted.

"My dear Miss Elinor, he was probably born in some Kansas cabin and has practiced killing snakes all his life. Not a very elevating feat. Let's go down and explore Lagonda Ledge now before the other snake comes in for the coroner's inquest."

And the two passed down the stone steps to the shady level campus and on to the town beyond it.

"You are hard on snakes, Burleigh," Dr. Fenneben said as he welcomed the country boy into his study. "A bull snake is a harmless creature, and he is the farmer's friend."

"Let him stay on the farm then. I hate him. He's no friend of mine," Vic replied.

He was overflowing the chair recently graced by Professor Burgess and clutching his derby as if it might escape and leave him bareheaded forever. His face had a dogged expression and his glance was stern. Yet his direct words and the deep richness of his voice put him outside of the class of commonplace beginners.

"Are you fond of killing things?" the Dean asked.

The ruddy color deepened in Vic Burleigh's brown cheek, but the steadfast gaze of his eyes and the firm lines of his mouth told the head of Sunrise something of what he would find in the sturdy young Jayhawker.

"Sometimes," came the blunt answer. "I've always lived on a Kansas claim. Unless you know what that means you might not understand—how hard a life"—Vic stopped abruptly and squeezed the rim of his derby.

"Never mind. We take only face value here. Fine view from that window," and Lloyd Fenneben's genial smile began to win the heart of the country boy as most young hearts were won to him.

Burleigh leaned toward the window, forgetful of the chair arms he had striven to subdue, the late afternoon sunlight falling on his brown face and glinting in his auburn hair.

"It's as pretty as paradise," he said, simply. "There's nothing like our Kansas prairies."

"You come from the plains out west, I hear. How long do you plan to stay here, Burleigh?" Dr. Fenneben asked.

"Four years if I can make it go. I've got a little schooling and I know how to herd cattle. I need more than this, if I am only a country boy."

"Who pays for your schooling, yourself, or your father?" Fenneben queried.

"I have no father nor mother now."

"You are willing to work four years to get a diploma from Sunrise? It is hard work; all the harder if you have not had much schooling before it."

"I'm willing to work, and I'd like to have the diploma for it," Vic answered.

"Burleigh, did you notice the letter S carved in the stone above the door?"

"Yes, sir; I suppose it stands for Sunrise?"

"It does. But with the years it will take on new meanings for you. When you have learned all these meanings you will be ready for your diploma—and more. You will be far on your way to the winning of a Master's Degree."

Vic's eyes widened with a sort of child-like simplicity. He forgot his hat and the chair arms, and Dr. Fenneben noted for the first time that his golden-brown eyes matching his auburn hair were shaded by long black lashes, the kind artists rave about, and arched over with black brows.

"His eyes and voice are all right," was the Dean's mental comment. "There's good blood in his veins, I'll wager."

But before he could speak further the shrill scream of a frightened child came from the campus below the ridge. At the cry Vic Burleigh sprang to his feet, upsetting his chair, and without stopping to pick it up, he rushed from the building.

As he tore down the long flight of steps, Lloyd Fenneben caught sight of a child on the level campus running toward him as fast as its fat little legs could toddle. Two minutes later Vic Burleigh was back in the study, panting and hot, with the little one clinging to his neck.

"Excuse me, please," Vic said as he lifted the fallen chair. "I forgot all about Bug down there, and the widow Bull" —he gave a half-smile— "was wriggling around trying to find her mate, and scared him. He's too little to be left alone, anyhow."

Bug was a sturdy, stubby three-year-old, or less, dimpled and brown, with big dark eyes and a tangle of soft little red-brown ringlets. As Vic seated himself, Bug perched on the arm of the chair inside of the big boy's encircling arm.

"Who is your friend? Is he your brother?" asked the Dean.

"No. He's no relation. I don't know anything about him, except that his name is Buler. Bug Buler, he says."

Little Bug put up a chubby brown hand loving-wise to Vic Burleigh's brown cheek, and, looking straight at Dr. Fenneben with wide serious eyes, he asked,

"Is you dood to Vic?"

"Yes, indeed," replied the Dean.

"Nen, I like you fornever," Bug declared, shutting his lips so tightly that his checks puffed.

"How do you happen to have this child here, Burleigh?" questioned Fenneben.

"Because he's got nobody else to look after him," answered Vic.

"How about an orphan asylum?"

Vic looked down at the little fellow cuddled against his arm, and every feature of his stern face softened.

"Will it make any difference about him if I get my lessons, sir? I can't let Bug go now. We are the limit for each other—neither of us got anybody else. I take care of him, but he keeps me from getting too coarse and rough. Every fellow needs something innocent and good about him sometimes."

"Oh, no! Keep him if you want him. But would you mind telling me about him?"

"I'd rather not now," Burleigh said, quietly, and Lloyd Fenneben knew when to drop a subject.

"Then I'm through with you for today, Burleigh. I must let Miss Saxon have my room now. Come here whenever you like, and bring Bug if you care to."

Sunrise students always left Dr. Fenneben's study with a little more of self-respect than when they entered it; richer, not so much from the word as from the spirit of the head of Sunrise. Victor Burleigh with little Bug Buler's fat fist clasped in his big, hard hand walked out of the college door that afternoon with the unconscious baptism of the student upon him, the dim sense of a fellowship with a scholarly master of books and of men.

Back in his study Lloyd Fenneben sat looking out once more at the Empire that meant nothing but dreary distances to the scholarly professor of Greek, and seemed a paradise to the untrained young fellow from the prairies.

"I see my stint of cloth for the day," he murmured. "A college professor in the making who has much to unlearn; a crude young giant who is fond of killing things, and cares for helpless children; and a beautiful, wilful, characterless girl to be shown into her womanly heritage. The clay is ready. It is the potter whose hands need skill. Victor Burleigh! Victor Burleigh! There's my greatest problem of all three. He has the strength of a Titan in those arms, and the passion of a tiger behind those innocent yellow eyes. God keep me on the hilltop nor let my feet once get into the dark and dangerous ways!"

He looked long at the landscape radiant under the level rays of splendor streaming from the low afternoon sun.

"I wonder who built that fire, and what that pillar of smoke meant this afternoon. The mystery of our lives hangs some token in each day."

The shadows were gathering in the Walnut Valley, the pigeons about the cottage up the river, were in their cotes now, the heat of the day was over, and with one more look at the far peaceful prairies Dr. Lloyd Fenneben closed his study door and passed out into the cool September air.

## CHAPTER III. PIGEON PLACE

Strange is the wind and the tide,
The heavens eternally wide;
Less fathomed, this life at my side.
      —W. H. SIMPSON

THE Sunrise rotunda was ringing with a chorus from three hundred throats as three hundred students poured out of doors, and over-flowed the ridge and spilled down the broad steps, making a babel of musical tongues; while fitting itself to every catchy college air known to Sunrise came the noisy refrain:

    Rah for Funnybone!
    Rah for Funnybone!
    Rah for Funnybone!
    Rah! RAH! RAH!!!

Again it was repeated, swelling along the ridge and floating wide away over the Walnut Valley. Nor was there a climax of exuberance until the appearance of Dr. Lloyd Fenneben himself, with his tall figure and striking presence outlined against the gray stone columns of the veranda. All this because it was mid-October, a heaven-made autumn day in Kansas, with its gracious warmth and bracing breath; with the Indian summer haze in shimmering amethyst and gold overhanging the land; and the Walnut Valley, gorgeous in the glow of the October frost-fires, winding down between broad seas of rainbow-radiant prairies. And all this gladness and grandeur, by the decree of Dr. Fenneben, was given in fee simple to these three hundred young people for the hours of one perfect day—their annual autumn holiday. No wonder they filled the air with shouts. And before the singing had ceased the crowd broke into groups by natural selection, and the holiday was begun.

Whatever bounds of time Nature may give to the seed in which to become a plant, or to the grub to become a butterfly, there is no set limit wherein the country-bred boy may bloom into a full-fledged college student.

Seven weeks after Vic Burleigh had come alongside the Greek Professor into Sunrise, found the quick marvelous change from the timid, untrained, overgrown young giant into a leader of his clan, the pride of the Freshman, the terror of the Sophomores, the dramatic interest of the classroom, and the hope of Sunrise on the football gridiron. His store-made clothes had a jaunty carelessness of fit. The tan had left his cheek. His auburn hair had lost its sun-burn. His powerful physique, the charm of his deep voice, the singular beauty of his wide open golden-brown eyes, with their long black lashes lighting up his rugged face, gave to him an attractive personality.

Yet to Lloyd Fenneben, who saw below the surface, Victor Burleigh was only at the beginning of things. Something of the tiger light in the brown eyes, the pride in brute strength, the blunt justice lacking the finer sense of mercy, showed how wide yet was the distance between the man and the gentleman.

When Dr. Fenneben returned to his study after the hilarious demonstration he found Dennie Saxon busy with the little film of dust that comes in overnight. Old Bond Saxon, Dennie's father, had been one of the improvident of Lagonda Ledge who took a new lease on a livelihood with the advent of Sunrise. From being a dissipated old fellow drifting toward pauperism, he became the proprietor of a respectable boarding house for students, doing average well. At rare intervals, however, he lapsed into his old ways. During such occasions he kept to the river side of the town. Sober, he was good-natured and obliging; drunken, he was sullen, with a disposition to skulk out of sight and be alone. His daughter Dennie had her father's good-nature combined with a will power all her own.

As Dr. Fenneben watched her about her work this morning, he noted how comfortably she took hold of it. He noted, too, that her heavy yellow-brown hair was full of ripples just where ripples helped, that her arms were plump, that she was short and nothing willowy, and that she had a mischievous twinkle in her eyes.

"Why don't you take a holiday, Miss Dennie?" he asked, presently.

"I wanted this done so I wouldn't be seeing dusty books in my daydreams," Dennie answered.

"Where do you do your dreaming today?"

"A crowd of us are going down the river to the Kickapoo Corral. I must make the cakes yet this morning," she answered.

"Good enough Can't I do something for you? Do you need a chaperon?" the Dean queried, smilingly.

"Professor Burgess is to be our chaperon. He is all we can look after." Dennie's gray eyes danced, but she was serious a moment later.

"Dr. Fenneben, you can do something, maybe, that's none of your business, nor mine." Dennie wondered afterward how she could have had the courage to speak these words.

"That's generally the easy thing. What is it?" the Dean smiled.

The girl hung her feather brush in its place and sat down opposite to him.

"Do you know anything about Pigeon Place?" she began.

"The little place up the river where a queer, half-crazy woman lives alone with a fierce dog?" he asked.

"Yes, you never heard anything more?" Dennie queried.

"Only that the house is hidden from the road and has many pigeons about it, and that the woman sees few callers. I've never located the place. Tell me about it," he replied.

"Bug Buler and I were up there after eggs this morning. Bug is Victor Burleigh's little boy. They board at our house," Dennie explained. "Pigeon Place is a little cottage all covered with vines and with flowers everywhere. It's hidden away from the road just outside of town. Mrs. Marian isn't crazy nor queer, only she seldom leaves home, never goes to church, nor visits anywhere. She doesn't care for anybody, nor take any interest in Lagonda Ledge, and she keeps a Great Dane dog, as big as a calf, that is friendly to women and children, but won't let a man come near, unless Mrs. Marian says so." Dennie paused.

"Very interesting, Miss Dennie, but what can I do?" Fenneben asked. "Shall I kill the dog and carry off the woman like the regulation grim ogre of the fairy tales?"

Dennie hesitated. Few girls would have come to a college president on such a mission as hers. But then few college presidents are like Lloyd Fenneben.

"Of course nobody likes Mrs. Marian, and my father—when he's not quite himself—says dreadful things if I mention her name." Dennie's checks were crimson as she thought of her father. "It's none of my business, but I've felt sorry for Mrs. Marian ever since she came here. She seems like an innocent outcast."

"That is very pitiful." Lloyd Fenneben's voice was sympathetic.

"This morning," continued Dennie, "Bug was playing with the dog outside, and I went into the house for the first time. Mrs. Marian is very pleasant. She asked me about my work here and I told her about Sunrise and you, and your niece, Miss Elinor, being here."

"All the interesting features. Did you mention Professor Burgess?" The query was innocently meant, but it brought the color to Dennie Saxon's cheek.

"No, I didn't think he was in that class," she replied, quickly. "But what surprised me was her interest in things. She is a pretty, refined, young-looking woman, with gray hair. When I was leaving I turned back to ask about some eggs for Saturday. She thought I was gone, and she had dropped her head on the table and was crying, so I slipped out without her knowing." Dennie's gray eyes were full of tears now. "Dr. Fenneben, if talking about Sunrise made her do that, maybe you might do something for her. I pity her so. Nobody seems to care about her. My father is set against her when he is not responsible, and he might—" She stopped abruptly and did not finish the sentence.

The Dean looked out of the window at the purple mist melting along the horizon line. Down in the valley pigeons were circling above a wooded spot at a bend in the Walnut River. Fenneben remembered now that he had seen them there many times. He had a boyhood memory of a country home with pigeons flying about it.

"I wish, too, that I might do something," he said at last. "You say she will not let men inside her gate now. I'll keep her in mind, though. The gate may open some time."

It was mid-afternoon when Lloyd Fenneben left his study for a stroll. As he approached the Saxon House, he saw old Bond Saxon slipping out of the side gate and with uncertain steps skulk down the alley.

"Poor old sinner! What a slave and a fool whisky can make of a man!" he thought. Then he remembered Dennie's anxiety of the morning. "There must be some cause for his prejudice against this strange hermit woman when he is drunk. Bond Saxon is not a man to hate anybody when he is sober."

"Is you Don Fonnybone?" Bug Buler's little piping voice from the doorstep haled the Dean. "I finked Vic would turn, and he don't turn, and I 's hungry for somebody. May I go wis you, Don Fonnybone?" The baby lips quivered.

Lloyd Fenneben held out his hand and Bug put his little fist into it.

"Where shall we go, Bug? I 'm hungry for somebody, too."

"Let's do find the bunny the bid dod ist scared away this morning. Turn on!"

Lloyd Fenneben was hardly conscious that Bug was choosing their path as the two strolled away together. Everywhere there was the pathos of a waning autumn day, and a soft haze creeping out of the west was making a blood-red carbuncle of the sun, set as a jewel on the amber-veiled bosom of the sky. The air was soft, wooing the spirit to a still, sweet peace. The two were at the outskirts of Lagonda Ledge now. The last board walk was three blocks back, and the cinder-made way had dwindled to a bare hard path by the roadside. A bend in the river cutting close to the road shows a long vista of the

Walnut bordered by vine-draped shrubbery and overhung with trees. A slab of limestone beside a huge elm tree had been placed at this bend to prevent the bank from breaking, or a chance misdriving into the water.

"I 's pitty tired," Bug said as the two reached the stone. "Will we tum to the bunny's house pitty soon?"

"We'll rest here a while and maybe the bunny will come out to meet us," Dr. Fenneben said, and they sat down on the broad stone.

"It was somewhere here the bunny runned." Little Bug studied the roadside with a quaint puzzled face. "Is you 'faid of snakes?"

"Not very much." The Dean's eyes were on the graceful flight of pigeons circling about the trees beyond the bend.

"Vic isn't 'faid. He killed bid one, two, five, free wattle, wattle snakes—" Bug caught his breath suddenly—"He told me not to tell that. I fordot. I don't 'member. He didn't do it—he didn't killed no snakes fornever."

Dr. Fenneben gave little heed to this prattle. His eyes were on the pigeons cleaving the air with short, graceful flights. Presently he felt the soft touch of baby curls against his hand, and little Bug had fallen asleep with his drooping head on Fenneben's lap.

The Dean gently placed the tired little one in an easy position, and rested his shoulder against the tree.

"That must be Pigeon Place," he mused. "Every town has its odd characters. This is one of Lagonda Ledge's little mysteries. Dennie finds it a pathetic one. How graceful those pigeons are!" And his thoughts drifted to a far New England homestead where pigeons used to sweep about an old barn roof.

A fuzzy gray rabbit flashed across the road, followed by a Great Dane dog in hot chase.

"Bug's bunny! I hope the big murderer will miss it," Fenneben thought.

The roadside bushes half hid him. As the crashing sound of the huge dog through the underbrush ceased he noticed a woman coming leisurely toward him. Her arms were full of bitter-sweet berries and flaming autumn leaves. She wore no hat and Fenneben saw that her gray hair was wound like a coronal about her head. Before he could catch sight of her face a heavy staggering step was beside him, and old Bond Saxon, muttering and shaking his clenched fists, passed beyond him toward the woman. Lloyd Fenneben's own fists clenched, but he sat stone still. The woman seemed to melt into the bushes and obliterate herself entirely, while the drunken man stalked unsteadily on toward where she had been. Then shaking his fists vehemently at the pigeons, he skulked around the bend in the road.

As soon as he was out of sight the woman emerged from the bushes, with autumn leaves hiding her crown of hair. She hastened a few rods toward the man watching her, then disappeared through a vine-covered gateway into a wilderness of shrubbery, beyond which the pigeons were cooing about their cotes.

As she closed the gate, she caught sight of Lloyd Fenneben, leaning motionless against the gray bole of the elm tree. But she was looking through a tangle of purple oak leaves and twining bitter-sweet branches, and Fenneben was unconscious of being discovered.

"A woman never could whistle," he smiled, as he listened, "but that call seems to do for the dog, all right."

The Great Dane was tearing across lots in answer to the trill of a woman's voice.

"She is safe now. But what does it all mean? Is there a wayside tragedy here that calls for my unraveling?"

Attracted by some subtle force beyond his power to check, he turned toward the river and looked steadily at the still overhanging shrubbery. Just below him, where the current turns, the quiet waters were lapping about a ledge of rock. Between that ledge and himself a tangle of bushes clutched the steep bank. He looked straight into the tangle, just plain twig and brown leaf, giving place as he stared, for two still black human eyes looking balefully at him as a snake at its prey. Lloyd Fenneben could not withdraw his gaze. The two eyes— no other human token visible—just two cruel human eyes full of human hate were fixed on him. And the fascination of the thing was paralyzing, horrible. He could not move nor utter a sound. Bug Buler woke with a little cry. The bushes by the riverside just rippled—one quiver of motion—and the eyes were not there. Then Fenneben knew that his heart, which had been still for an age, had begun to beat again. Bug stared up into his face, dazed from sleep.

"Where's my Vic? Who's dot me?" he cried.

"We came to hunt the bunny. He's gone away again. Shall we go back home?" The gentle voice and strong hand soothed the little one.

"It's dettin' told. Let's wun home." Bug cuddled against Fenneben's side and hugged his hand. "I love you lots," he said, looking up with eyes of innocent trust.

"Yes, let's run home. There is a storm in the air and the sun is hidden from the valley." He stooped and kissed the little upturned face. "Thank heaven for children!" he murmured. "Amid skulking, drunken men and strange, lonely women, and cruel eyes of unknown beings, they lead us loving-wise back home again."

Behind the vine-covered gate a gray-haired, fair-faced woman watched the two as they disappeared down the road.

And the blood-red sun out on the west prairie sank swiftly into a blue cloudbank, presaging the coming of a storm.

## CHAPTER IV. THE KICKAPOO CORRAL

And even now, as the night comes, and the shadows gather round,
And you tell the old-time story, I can almost hear the sound
Of the horses' hoofs in the silence, and the voices of struggling men;
For the night is the same forever, and the time comes back again.
            —JAMES W. STEELE

FROM the beginning of things in the Walnut Valley, the Kickapoo Corral had its uses. Nature built it to this end. The river course follows the pattern of the letter S faced westward instead of eastward. The upper half of the letter is properly shaped, but the sharpened curve at the middle leaves only a narrow distance across the lower space. In this outline runs the Walnut, its upper curve almost surrounding a little wooded peninsula that slopes gently on its side to the water's edge. But the farther bank stands up in a straight limestone bluff forming a high wall of protection about the river-encircled ground. A less severe bluff crosses the open part of the peninsula, reaching the hither side of the river below the sharp bend. The space inside, stone-walled and water-bound, made an ideal shelter for the wild life that should inhabit it. And Nature saw that it was good and went away and left it, not forgetting to lock the door upon it. For the enemy who would enter this protecting shelter must come through the gateway of the river. There was only one right place to do this. Deceivingly near to the shallow rock-based ford before the Corral, so near that only the wise ones knew how to miss it, Nature placed the cruelest whirlpool that ever swung an even surface up stream, its gentle motion telling nothing of the fatal suction underneath that level stretch of steady, slow moving, irresistible water.

What use the primitive tribes made of this spot the river has never told. But in the day of the Kickapoo supremacy it came to its christening. Here the tribe found a refuge and harbored its stolen plunder. From this wooded covert it sent its death-singing arrows through the heart of its enemy who dared to stand in relief on that stone bluff. Here it laughed at the drowning cries of those who were caught in the fatal whirlpool beyond the curve in the river wall, and here it endured siege and slaughter when foes were valiant enough, and numerous enough to storm into its stronghold over the dead bodies of their own vanguard.

Weird and tragical are the legends of the Kickapoo Corral, left for a stronger race to marvel over. For, with the swing of time, the white man cut a road down the steep bluff at the sharpest bend and made a ford in the shallow place between the whirlpool and the old Corral, and the Nature-built stockade became a peaceful spot, specially ordained by Providence, the Sunrise Freshmen claimed, as a picnic ground for their autumn holiday. At least the young folk for whom Professor Burgess was acting as chaperon took it so, and reveled in the right.

Interest in Greek had greatly increased in Sunrise with the advent of the handsome young Harvard man, and his desired seclusion for profound research had not yet been fully realized. Types for study were plentiful, however, especially the type of the presumptuous young fellow who dared to admire Elinor Wream. By divine right she was the most popular girl in Sunrise, which pleased Professor Burgess up to a certain point. That point was Victor Burleigh. The silent antagonism between these two daily grew stronger; why, neither one could have told up to this holiday.

The day had been perfect—the weather, the dinner, the company, the woodland—even the amber light in the sky softening the glow as the afternoon slipped down toward twilight in the sheltered old Corral.

"Come, Vic Burleigh, help me to start this fire for supper," Dennie Saxon called. "We won't get our coffee and ham and eggs ready before midnight."

"Here, Trench, or some of you fellows, get busy," Vic called back to the big right guard of the Sunrise football squad. "Elinor and I are going to climb the west bluff to see what's the matter with the sun. It looks sick. I've been hired man all day; carried nineteen girls across the shallows, packed all the lunch-baskets, toted all the wood, built all the fires, washed all the dishes—"

"Ate all the dinner, drank all the grape juice, stepped on all the custard pies, upset all the cream bottles. Oh, you piker, get out!" Trench aimed an empty lunch-basket at Vic's head with the words.

Being a chaperon was a pleasant office to Professor Burgess today but for the task of throwing a barrier about Elinor every time Vic Burleigh came near. And Burleigh, lacking many other things more than insight, kept him busy at barrier building.

"Miss Wream, you can't think of climbing that rough place," Burgess protested, with a sharp glance of resentment at the big young fellow who dared to call her Elinor.

The tiger-light blazed in the eyes that flashed back at him, as Vic cried daringly.

"Oh, come on, Elinor; be a good Indian!"

"Don't do it, Miss Wream," Vincent Burgess pleaded.

Elinor looked from the one to the other, and the very magnetism of power called her.

"I mean to try, anyhow," she declared. "Will you pick me up if I fall, Victor?"

"Well, I wouldn't hardly go away and leave you to perish miserably," Vic assured her, and they were off together.

The Wream men were slender, and all of them, except Lloyd Fenneben, the stepbrother, wore nose glasses and drank hot water at breakfast, and ate predigested foods, and talked of acids and carbons, and took prescribed gestures for exercise. The joyousness of perfect health was in every motion of this young man. His brown sweater showed a hard white throat. He planted his feet firmly. And he leaped up the bluffside easily. If Elinor slipped, the strength of his grip on her arm reassured her, until climbing beside him became a joy.

The bluff was less surly than it appeared to be down in the Corral, and the benediction of autumn was in the view from its crest. They sat down on the stone ledge crowning it, and Elinor threw aside her jaunty scarlet outing cap. The breezes played in her dark hair, and her cheeks were pink from the exercise. Victor Burleigh looked at her with frank, wide-open eyes.

"What's the matter? Is my hair a fright?" she murmured.

"A fright!" Burleigh flung off his cap and ran his fingers through his own hair. "Not what I call a fright," he asserted in an even tone.

"What's that scar on your left arm? It looks like a little hole dug out," Elinor declared.

Vic's brown sweater sleeve was pushed up to the elbow.

"It is a little hole I put in where I dug out the flesh with a pocket knife," he replied, carelessly.

"Did you do that yourself?" Elinor cried. "What made you be so cruel?"

"I wasn't so cruel. 'I seen my duty and I done it noble,' as the essay runs. I made that vacancy to get ahead of a rattlesnake that got me there, a venomous big one with nine police calls on its tail, and that's no snake story, either. I cut the flesh out to get rid of the poison. I was n't in a college laboratory and I had to work fast and use what tools I had with me. I killed the gentleman that did the mischief, though," Vic added carelessly, deftly slipping down his sleeve as if to change the subject.

"Oh, tell me about it, do," Elinor urged. "You were killing a snake the first time I saw you."

How dainty and sweet she was sitting there in her neat-fitting outing suit of dark gray with scarlet pipings and buttons and pocket flaps, and the scarlet of her full lips, and the coral tint of her cheeks, the white hands and white throat and brow, the dark eyes and finely shaped head with abundant beautiful hair.

Vic Burleigh sat looking straight at her and the light in his own eyes told nothing of the glitter that had flashed in them when he glared at Professor Burgess down in the Corral.

"I wasn't killing snakes. I was looking up at a girl on the rotunda stairs the first time," he said, "and I don't want to tell about this scar, because I've wished a thousand times to forget it. See how much darker it is down there than it is up here."

The shadows were lengthening in the Corral where the supper fires were gleaming. Across the low bluff the imprisoned sun was sending a dull red glow along the waters of the Walnut.

"Look at that still place in the river, Victor. The ripples are all on the farther side," Elinor said, looking pensively downstream.

"Watch it a minute. Do you see that bit of drift coming upstream in the still water?" Vic asked.

"Why, the water does move; toward us, too, instead of down the river. I'd like to boat around in that quiet place."

She was leaning forward, resting her chin in her hand. In outline against the misty background shot through with the crimson light from the storm-smothered sun, with the gray shadows of the old Kickapoo Corral below them, hemmed in by the silver gleaming waters of the Walnut, a picture grew up before Victor Burleigh's eyes that he was never to forget. Like the cleft of the lightning through the cloud, like the flash of the swallow's wing, the careless-hearted boy leaped to the stature of a man, into whose soul the love of a lifetime is born. Unconsciously, he drew away from her, and long afterward she recalled the sweetness of his deep voice when he spoke again.

"Elinor Wream, I'd rather see you helpless up here with the hungriest wild beast between us that ever tore a human form to pieces than to see you in that quiet water below the shallows."

"Why?" Elinor looked up into his face.

"Because I could save your life here, maybe, even if I lost mine. Down there I could drown for you, but that would n't save you. Nobody ever swam that whirlpool and lived to tell about it. There's a ledge underneath that holds down what the infernal slow suction swallows. But it's dead sure."

"Why, that's awful," Elinor said, lightly, for she had no picture of him engulfed in the slow-moving treachery below them.

"There's an old Indian legend about that pool," Vic said, staring down at the water.

"Tell me about it." Elinor was breaking the twigs from a branch of buck-berry growing beside her.

"Oh, it's a tragical one, like everything else about that place," Vic responded, grimly. "Old Lagonda, Chief of the Wahoos, I reckon, I don't know his tribe, did n't want to give up this valley to the sons and heirs of Sunrise to desecrate with salmon cans and pop bottles and Harvard-turned chaperons. He held out against putting his multiplication sign to the treaty, claiming that land was like water and air and could n't be bought and sold. But the white men with true missionary courtesy held his head under water till he burbled 'Nuff,' and signed up with a piece of charcoal. Then he went down the river to this smooth-faced whirlpool, and laid a curse on the sons of men who had taken his own from him."

The twilight had deepened. The sun was lost in the cloudbank out of which a hot wind was sweeping eastward. Vic was telling the story well, and the magnetism of his voice was compelling. Elinor drew nearer to him.

"What was the curse? I would n't want to go near that place, unless you were with me."

The very innocence of the words put a thrill in Vic Burleigh's every pulse beat.

"Don't ever do it, if you can help it." Vic could not keep back the words. "Old Lagonda decreed a tribute to the river for the wrong done to him, a life a year in that pool. And the Walnut has been exacting in its rights. Life after life has gone out down there until sometimes it seems like the old chief's curse would never be lifted."

"I hope it may be, while I am at Sunrise, anyhow," Elinor said. "I don't like real tragedies about me. I like an easy, comfortable life, and everybody good and happy. I hope the curse will be staid until I go back home."

Vic hadn't thought of this. Of course, she would leave Sunrise some time. Her home was in Cambridge-by-the-Sea, not on the Prairie-by-the-Walnut. She belonged to the dead-language scholars, not to crude red-blooded creatures like himself. He turned his face to the west and the threatening sky seemed in harmony with his storm-riven soul. He was so young—less than half an hour older than the big whole-hearted fellow who started up the bluff in picnic frolic with a pretty girl whom Professor Burgess adored. That was one reason why he had brought her up. He wanted to tease the Professor then. He hated Burgess now, and the white teeth clinched at the thought of him.

A sudden shouting and beating of tom-toms down in the Corral, and the call in crude rhyme to straggling couples to close in, announced supper. High above other whooping the voice of Trench, the big right guard, reached the top of the bluff:

> Victor Burleigh and Elinor Wream,
> Better wake from Love's Young Dream,
> Before the ants get into the cream.

The beating of a dishpan drowned the chorus. Then down by the river Dennie's soprano streamed out,

> The sun is sot,
> The coffee's hot,
> The supper's got.
>    What?
>   Yes! Got!

Answering this call from the north end of the Corral, a heavy base growled,

> Dennie is sad,
> The eggs are bad;
> The Professor's mad
> At a College lad.
> Burleigh! Burly! Burlee!

Come home! Come home! Come home!

"The Kickapoos are on the warpath. Let's go down and get into the running."

Vic lifted Elinor to her feet with a sort of reverence in his touch. But she did not note that it was otherwise than the good-natured grip of the comrade who had helped her up the steep places half an hour ago.

Descent was more difficult, and it was growing dark rapidly. Vic held her arm to keep her from falling, and once on a sliding rock, he had to catch both of her hands, and half-lift her to solid footing. Her shining eyes, starbright in the gloom, the dainty rose hue of her cheeks, the touch of her soft white hands, and her need for his strength, made the shadowy path delicious for her companion.

The call of the wild was in that evening camp in the autumn woodland, in the charm of the deepening twilight warmed with the red glow of the fires, in the appetizing odor of coffee, the unconventional freedom, the carelessness of youth, the jolly good-fellowship of comrades. To Professor Burgess it had the added charm of newness. All the pleasures of popularity were his this evening, for he was young himself, he dressed well, and he had the grace of a gentleman. The enjoyment of the day gave him a thrill of surprise. He was already dropping the viewpoint of Dr. Joshua Wream for Dean Fenneben's angle of vision. And in these picturesque surroundings he forgot about the weather and the prudence of getting home early.

"Throw that log on the fire, Vic. It begins to look spooky back here. I've just had my ear to the ground and I heard an awful roaring somewhere." Trench, who had been sprawling lazily in the shadows, now declared, "Say, I'd hate to be penned into this place so I couldn't get out. There's no skinning up that rock wall even if a fellow could swim the river, and I can't," and the big guard stretched himself on the ground again.

"What's that old story about the Kickapoos here?" somebody asked. "Dennie Saxon knows it. Tell us about it, Dennie, AND THEN WE'LL ALL GO HOME." The last words were half-sung.

"Be swift, Dennie, be quite swift. I heard that noise again. I'm afraid it's a stampede of wild horses." Trench, who had had his ear to the ground, sat up suddenly. But nobody paid any attention to him.

"Come, Denmark Saxon, let's close the day in song and story. You tell the story and then I'll sing the song," somebody declared.

"Aw-w-w!" a prolonged chorus. "Make your story long, Dennie; make it lengthy."

"Don't you do it, Dennie. I tell you this ground is shaking. I feel it," Trench insisted.

"Say, who's got the bromo-seltzer? The right guard's supper is n't treating him right. Go ahead, Dennie," the crowd urged.

They were all in a circle about the fire. Its flickering glow lighted Vic Burleigh's rugged face, and gleamed in his auburn hair. Elinor sat between him and Vincent Burgess. Dennie was just beyond Vincent, who noted incidentally the play of light and shadow on the blowsy ripples of her hair that night and remembered it all on a day long afterward.

"Once upon a time," Dennie began,

there was a beautiful Kickapoo Indian maiden—"

"Yep, any Kickapoo's a beaut. Hurry up, Dennie. I hear something coming." It was the big lazy guard again.

"Oh! Vic Burleigh, sit on his prostrate form. Go on, Dennie," the company insisted, and she continued.

"Her name was The Fawn of the Morning Light, her best lover was Swift Elk."

"You be Mrs. Swift Elk—" but Vic Burleigh's arm about Trench's throat choked his words.

"And there was a wily Sioux, named Red Fox, who loved the Fawn and wanted her to marry him. She wouldn't do it. The Kickapoos were heap-big grafters, and they had this old Corral full of ponies and junk they had relieved other tribes of caring for. And the only way to get in here, besides falling over the bluff and becoming a pin-cushion for poisoned arrows, was to come in by the shallows in the river where the ford is now above old Lagonda's pool, and most Indians needed a diagram for that." Although Dennie spoke lightly, she shuddered a little at the thought, and the whole company grew graver.

"An Indian doesn't forget. So, Red Fox, who had sworn to have The Fawn, came down here with hundreds of Sioux who wanted the ponies the Kickapoos had stolen, as Red Fox wanted Swift Elk's girl. The Kickapoos wouldn't give up the ponies and Swift Elk wouldn't give up The Fawn. So the siege began. Right where we are so safe and peaceful tonight those Kickapoos fought, and starved, and died, while the Sioux kept cruel watch on the top of that old stone ledge, never letting one escape. At last, after hours and hours of siege, The Fawn and Swift Elk decided to escape by the river in the night. A storm had come on suddenly, and a cloudburst up the Walnut was sending a perfect surge of water down around the bend. The two lovers were caught in its sweep and carried beyond the shallows when a flash of lightning showed them to Red Fox watching on the bluff up there. At the next flash he sent an arrow straight through Swift Elk's body and into The Fawn's shoulder, pinning the two together. The Sioux leaped into the stream to save the girl he loved, but the heavy current swept them toward the whirlpool, and before they could prevent the dying and wounded and rescuing were all caught by the fatal suction. Then the Sioux warriors rushed in from all sides, upstream, down the bluff from west prairie, and over the Corral, and slaughtered every Kickapoo here. Their fierce yells and the shrieks of the squaws and pappooses, the pounding of horses' hoofs in the stampede of hundreds of ponies, the roar of the river, the wrath of the storm made a scene this old Corral will never see again." Dennie paused.

"I think I hear something like it, right now," came Trench's irrepressible voice from the shadows in the edge of the circle. But nobody heeded it.

And all the while from far across the west prairie the stormcloud was rolling in, black and angry, blowing its hot breath before it, while from a cloudburst upstream an hour before a great surge of water was rushing down the Walnut, turning the quiet river to a murderous flood. But the high walls hid all this from the valley and the heedless young folk took the full time limit of their holiday in the sheltering gloom of the old Kickapoo Corral.

## CHAPTER V. THE STORM

Rock and moan, and roar alone,
And the dread of some nameless thing unknown.
—LOWELL

THE silence following Dennie's story was broken by a sudden peal of thunder overhead. At the same instant the blackness of midnight lifted itself above the stone ledges and dropped down upon the Corral, smothering everything in darkness. A rushing whirlwind, a lurid blaze of lightning, and a second peal of thunder threw the camp into blind disorder. In the minute's lull following the first storm herald, there was a wild scrambling for wraps and lunch baskets. Then the darkness thickened and the storm's fury burst upon the crowd—a mad lashing of bending tree tops, a blinding whirl of dust filling the air, the thunder's terrific cannonade, the incessant blaze of lightning, the rattling of the distant rain; and above all these, unlike them all, a steady, dreadful roaring, coming nearer each moment.

Professor Burgess was no coward, but he had little power of generalship. As the crowd huddled together under the swaying trees, Trench called to Burleigh:

"There's been a cloudburst up stream. The roar I've been hearing is a wall of water coming down. We've got to get out of this."

Then above all the crashing and booming they heard Vic Burleigh's voice:

"Every fellow take a girl and run for the ford. Come on!"

In the darkness, each boy caught the arm of the girl nearest him and made a dash for the ford. A flash of lightning showed Burleigh that the white-faced girl clinging to his arm was Elinor Wream. After that, the storm was a plaything for him.

The first to reach the ford were Vincent Burgess and Dennie Saxon. Dennie was sure-footed and she knew by instinct where to find the shallows. But the river was rising rapidly and the waters were black and angry under the lightning's glitter. As the crowd held back Vic shouted:

"You'll have to wade. It's not very deep yet. Professor, you must cross first, and count 'em as they come. Go quick! One at a time. The way is narrow. And for God's sake, keep to the upper side of the shallows. Stand in the middle, Trench, and don't let them get down stream below you."

They were all safely across except Vic and Elinor, when Trench cried out:

"Send your girl in quick, Burleigh, and you run west. The flood is at the bend now. Hurry!"

"Run in, Elinor. Trench will take you through, and I'll follow, for I can swim and he can't. I'll be right behind you. Run!"

A vision of the whirlpool and of Swift Elk and The Fawn flashed into Elinor's mind, filling her with terror. Before Vic could push her forward, Trench shouted:

"It's too late. Don't try it. I've got to run."

He was strong and sure-footed and he fought his way gallantly to the further side as a great wave swirled around the curve of the river, engulfing the shallows in its mad surge. When he reached the east bank the count of the company numbered all but two.

"It's Vic and Elinor," Trench declared. "Vic wouldn't come till the last, and Elinor was too dead scared to trust anybody else, I guess. Nobody could cross there now, Professor. But Vic is as strong as an ox and he's not afraid of the devil. He'll keep both their heads above water. He wants to win out in the Thanksgiving game too much to get lost now. Trust him to get up the bluff some way, and back to town by the Main street bridge like as not, before we get there. There's no shelter between here and Lagonda Ledge. Let's all cut for it before the rain beats us into the mud."

The deluge was just beginning, so, safe, but wet, and mud-smeared, fighting wind and rain and darkness, taking it all as a jolly lark, although they had slidden into safety but a hand's breadth in front of death, the couples straggled back to town.

Vincent Burgess, anxious, angry, and jealous, found an unconscious comfort in Dennie Saxon in that homeward struggle. She was so capable and cheery that he forgot a little the girl who had as surely drawn him Kansas-ward as his interest in types and geographical breadth had done. It dimly entered his consciousness, as he told Dennie good-bye, that maybe she had been the most desirable companion of the crowd on such a night as this. He knew, at least, that he would have shown Elinor much more attention than he had shown to Dennie, and he knew that Elinor would have required it of him.

The light from the hall was streaming across the veranda of the Saxon House, a beam as faithful and friendly at the border of the lower campus as the bigger beacon in the college turret up on the lime-stone ridge. As Burgess started away the worst deluge of the night fell out of the sky, so he dropped down on a seat to wait for the downpour to weaken. He was very tired and his mind was feverishly busy. Where could Burleigh and Elinor be now? What dangers might threaten them? What ill might befall Elinor from exposure to this beating storm? He was frantic with the thought. Then he recalled Dennie, the girl who was working her way through college, whom he—Professor Vincent Burgess, A.B., from Harvard— had escorted home. How cheap Kansas was making him. The boys and girls had taken Dennie as one of them today; and truly, she did add to the comfort and pleasure of the outing. It seemed all right down in the woods where all was unconventional. But now, alone, in how common a grade he seemed to have placed himself, to be forced to pay attention to the poorest girl in school. His cheeks grew hot at the very thought of it.

In the shadows, beyond him, a form straightened up stupidly:

"Shay, Profesh Burgush, that you?"

Dennie's father, half-drunken still! Oh, Shades of classic culture! To what depths in social contact may a college man fall in this wretched land!

"Shay! Is't you, or ain't it you? You gonna tell me?" Old Bond queried.

"This is Vincent Burgess," the young man replied.

"Dennie home?" the father asked.

"Yes, sir," came the curt answer.

"Who? Who bring her home? Vic Burleigh?"

"I brought her home. She is a good girl, too."

In spite of himself, Burgess resented the shame of such a father for the capable, happy-spirited daughter.

"Yesh, Dennie's good girl, all right."

Then a silence fell.

Presently, the old man spoke again.

"Shay, Prof esh, 'd ye mind doin' somethin' for me?"

"What is it?" Burgess was by nature courteous.

"If anything sh'd ever happen to me, 'd you take care of Dennie? Shay, would you?"

"If I could do anything for her, I would do it," the young man replied.

"Somethin' gonna happen to me. I ain't shafe. I know I'll go that way. But you'll be good to Dennie. Now, wouldn't you? I'd ask Funnybone, but he's no shafer 'n I am. No shafer! You'll be good to Dennie, you said so. Shay it again!"

Bond was standing now bending threateningly toward Burgess, who had also risen.

"I'll do all that a gentleman ought to do." He had only one thought — to pacify the drunken man and get away. And the old man understood.

"Shwear it, I tell you! Lif' up your right hand an'—an' shwear to take care of Dennie, or I'll kill you!" Bond insisted.

He was a large, muscular man, towering over the slender young professor like a very giant, and in his eyes there was a cruel gleam. Vincent Burgess was at the limit of mental resistance. Lifting his shapely right hand in the shadowy light, he said wearily:

"I swear it!"

"One more question, and you may go. You know that little boy Vic Burleigh takes care of here?"

The Professor had heard of him.

"Vic keeps that little boy all right. He don't complain none. S'pose you help me watch um, Profesh." Then as an afterthought, Saxon added: "Young woman livin' out north of town. Pretty woman. She don't know nothing 'bout that little boy. Now, honest, she don't. Lives all by herself with a big dog."

Jealousy is an ugly, suspicious beast. Vincent Burgess was no worse than many other men would have been, because his mind leaped to the meaning old Saxon's words might carry. And this was the man with Elinor in the darkness and the storm. Before Burgess could think clearly, Saxon came a step nearer.

"Shay, where's Vic tonight?"

"Across the river with Miss Wream. They were cut off by the deep water," Vincent answered.

A quick change from drunkenness to sober sense leaped into Bond Saxon's eyes.

"Across the river! Great God!" Then sternly, with a grim set of jaw, he commanded: "You go home! If you dare to say a word, I'll kill you. If you try to follow me, he'll kill you. Go home! I 'm going over there, if I die for it." And the darkness and rain swallowed him as he leaped away to the westward!

44

Burgess gazed into the blackness into which Bond Saxon had gone until a soft hand touched his, and he looked down to see little Bug Buler, clad in his nightgown, standing barefoot beside him.

"Where's Vic?" Bug demanded.

"I don't know," Burgess answered.

"Take me up, I'se told." Bug stretched up his arms appealingly, and Burgess, who knew nothing of babies, awkwardly lifted him up.

"Tuddle me tlose like Vic do," and the little one snuggled lovingly in the Professor's embrace. "Your toat's wet. Is Vic wet, too?"

"Yes, little boy. We are all in trouble tonight." Burgess had to say something.

"In twouble? Umph—humph!" Bug shut his lips tightly, puffing out his cheeks, as was his habit. "I was in twouble, and I ist wented to Don Fonnybone. He's dood for twouble-ness. You go see him. Poor man!" and the little hand stroked Professor Burgess' feverish cheek.

"If you'll run right back to bed, I'll do it," Burgess declared. "We can learn even from children sometimes," he thought, as Bug climbed down obediently and toddled away.

Vincent Burgess went directly to Dr. Lloyd Fenneben, to whom he told the story of the day's events, including the interview with Bond Saxon. He did not repeat Bond's words regarding Vic, but only hinted at the suspicion that there was something questionable in the situation in which Vic was placed. Nor did he refer to the old man's maudlin demand that he should take care of Dennie if she were left fatherless, and of his sworn promise to do so.

Burgess felt as, if the Dean's black eyes would burn through him, so steady was their gaze while the story was being told. When he had finished, Lloyd Fenneben said quietly:

"You are worn out with the excitement of the day and night. Go home and rest now. I've learned through many a struggle, that what I cannot fight to a finish in the darkness, I can safely leave with God till the daylight comes."

The smile that lighted up the stern face and the firm handclasp with which Lloyd Fenneben dismissed the young man were things he remembered long afterward. And above all, he recalled many times a sense of secret shame that he should have felt degraded because of his association with Dennie Saxon on this day. But of this last, the memory was stronger than the present realization.

Meanwhile, as the mad waters surged around the bend in the river, and swept over the shallows, Victor Burleigh flung his arm around Elinor Wream and leaped back from the very edge of doom.

"We must climb the bluff again. Be a good Indian!" he cried, groping for a footing.

Climbing the west bluff by daylight for the sake of adventure was very unlike this struggle in the darkness to escape the widening river, with a wind-driven torrent of rain sweeping down the land behind the first storm-fury, and Elinor Wream clung to her companion's arm almost helpless with fear.

"Do you think you can ever get us out? she asked, as the limestone ledge blocked the way.

"Do you know what my mother named me?" The carelessness of the tone was surprising.

"Victor!" she replied.

"Then don't forget it," Burleigh said. "It's a dreadfully rough way before us, little girl, but we'll soon be safe from the river. Don't mind this little bit of a storm, and you'll get personally conducted into Lagonda Ledge before midnight."

In her sheltered life, Elinor had never known anything half so dreadful as this storm and darkness and booming flood, but the fearlessness of the strong man beside her inspired her to do her best. It was only two hours since they were here before. How could she know that these two hours had marked the crisis of a lifetime for Victor Burleigh. With a friendly little pressure on his arm, she said bravely:

"I'd rather be here with you than over the river with anybody else. I feel safer here."

Vic knew she meant only to be courteous, but the words were comforting. On the crest of the ledge the fierceness of the storm was revealed. Great sheets of wind-blown rain were flung athwart the landscape, and the utter blackness that followed the lightning's glare, and the roaring of the wind and river were appalling.

In all this tumult, away to the northeast, the beacon light above the Sunrise dome was cutting the darkness with a steady beam.

"See that light, Elinor? We are not lost. We must get up stream a little way. Then we'll find the bridge, all right. The crowd will get home ahead of us, because this is the rough side of the river."

"Oh, what a comfort a light can be!" Elinor murmured as she looked up and caught the welcome gleam.

As they hurried along, the Sunrise light suddenly disappeared and they found themselves descending a rough downward way. Presently there were rock walls on either side hemming them in a narrow crevice in the ledges. Then the rain ceased and Vic knew they had slidden down into a rock-covered fissure, that they were getting underground. They tried to turn back, but the up-climb was impossible, and in the darkness they could reach nothing but the sharp ledge of the cliff sheer above the raging river. Entrapped and bewildered, Vic felt cautiously about; but the only certain things were the straight bluff overhanging the flood, and the cavernous way leading downward; while the same deluge that was keeping Vincent Burgess storm-staid on the veranda of the Saxon House, was beating mercilessly down on Elinor Wream.

"We can't stay here and be threshed to pieces," Vic cried. "This crack is drier, anyhow, and it must lead to somewhere."

It did lead to what seemed to Elinor an endless length of hideous uncertainty, until Vic suddenly lost his footing and plunged headlong down somewhere into the blackness of darkness. Elinor shrieked in terror and sank down limply on the stone floor of the crevice.

"All a bluff," Vic called up cheerily, in the same startlingly deep sweet voice that had caught Elinor's ear on the September afternoon before the door of Sunrise, and out in the edge of her consciousness the thought played in again, "I'd rather be here with you than over the river with anybody else. I feel safer here."

"Slide down, Elinor. I'll catch you. It is n't very far, and there's a little light somewhere."

Elinor slipped blindly down the side of the rock into Vic Burleigh's outstretched arms. As he set her on her feet, somehow, the little light failed. In all their struggle, this part of the way seemed the darkest, the chillest, the most dangerous, and a sudden sense of a presence hidden nearby possessed them both, as they came against a blind wall. A stouter heart than Vic Burleigh's might well have quailed now. The two were lost underground. What deeper cavern might yawn beyond them? What length of dead wall might bar their way? And more terrifying still, was the growing sense of a human presence, a human menace, an unseen treachery. As Vic felt his way along the stone, his hand closed over something thrust into a little niche, shoulder-high in the wall. It seemed to be a small pitcher of unique pattern, solid silver by its weight. Was it the booty of some dead and forgotten robber chief, the buried treasure of some old Kickapoo raiding tragedy, or the loot of a living outlaw?

Vic thought he felt the outline of a letter graven in heavy relief on the smooth side, and, for a reason of his own, dropped the thing. Mercifully, he did not cry out at the discovery, but Elinor felt his hand on her arm grow chill.

A dazzling glare, token of the passing of the storm's fireworks, outlined an irregular opening in the wall before them, revealing at the same time a large room beyond the wall.

"Here's the hole where we get out of this trap, Elinor Wream. If such a big lightning like that can get in, we can get out," Vic cried.

He crawled through the opening, and pulled her as gently as possible after him. Presently, another blaze lit up the night outside, showing a cavern-like space thirty feet in dimensions, with a rock roof above their heads, and a low doorway through which the light from the outside had come in, and beyond which the rain was beating tremendously. Evidently they had found a rear entrance to this cavern.

"We are past our troubles now, Elinor," Vic said. "There's the real out-of-doors, and I feel sure of the rest of the way. This seems to be a sort of cave, and we have come in kind of irregularly by the back door or down the chimney. But here we are at the real front door. Shall we go on?"

Elinor leaned wearily against the wall, wet and cold, and almost exhausted.

"Let's wait a little, till this shower passes," she pleaded.

"You poor girl! This has been an awful night," Vic said gently.

Their eyes were getting accustomed to the darkness and they saw more clearly the outline of the opening to the outside world. Suddenly Elinor shivered as again the nearness of a presence somewhere possessed them both.

"Let's go! Let's go!" she whispered, huddling close to her companion, whose grip on her arm tightened.

He was conscious of a light behind him. Glancing over his shoulder, he caught a gleam beyond the opening in the rear wall through which they had just crept; and in that gleam, a villainous face, with still black eyes, looking straight at him. The light disappeared, and he heard the faint sound of something creeping toward them. Vic could fight any man living. Nature built him for that. He had no fear for himself. But here was Elinor, and he must think of her first. At that instant, the doorway darkened, and a form slipped into the cavern somewhere. Oh, wind and rain, and forked blue lightning and the thunder's roar, the river's mad floods, the steep, slippery rocks, and jagged ledges, all were kind beside this secret human presence, cruelly silent and treacherous.

Victor Burleigh drew Elinor closer to him, and whispered low:

"Don't be afraid with me to guard you."

Even in that deep gloom, he caught the outline of a white face with star-bright eyes lifted toward his face.

"I'm not afraid with you," she whispered.

Behind them stealthy movements somewhere. Between them and the doorway, stealthy movements somewhere; but all so still and slow, they stretched the listening nerve almost to the breaking point. Suddenly, a big, hard hand gripped Burleigh's shoulder, and a dead still voice, that Vic could not recognize, breathed into his ear, "Go quick and quiet! I'll stand for it. Go!"

It was old Bond Saxon.

Vic caught Elinor's arm, and with one stride they sprang from the cave's mouth up to the open ground beyond it. Something behind them, it might have been a groan or a smothered oath, reached their ears, as they sped away down a narrow ravine. The rain had ceased and overhead the stars were peeping from the edges of feathery flying clouds; and all the sodden autumn night was still at last, save for the gurgling waters of a little stream down the rocky glen.

The Sunrise bell was striking eleven when they reached the bridge across the Walnut, and the beacon light from the dome began to twinkle a welcome now and then through the dripping branches of the leafless trees. A few minutes later, Victor Burleigh brought Elinor safely to Lloyd Fenneben's door.

"We made it in before midnight, anyhow," he said carelessly.

Elinor looked up in surprise. The terrors of the night still possessed her.

"What a horrible nightmare it has all been. The storm, the river, the rocks, and the darkness, and that dreadful something behind us in the cave. Was there really anything, or did we just imagine it all? It will seem impossible when the daylight comes."

Victor looked at her with a wonderful light in his wide-open brown eyes.

"Yes," he said in a deep voice. "It will seem impossible when daylight comes. But will it all be as a horrible nightmare?"

"No, no; not all." Elinor's face was winsomely sweet. "Not all," she repeated. "It is fine to feel one's self so safeguarded as I have been. I shall always remember you as one with whom I could never again be afraid."

Burleigh turned hastily toward the door, and, having delivered her to the care of her uncle, he bade them both good night.

Dr. Fenneben looked keenly after the young man striding away from the light. His clothes were torn and bedraggled, his cap was gone, and his heavy hair was a mass of rough waves about his forehead. The direct gaze of his golden-brown eyes took away distrust, and yet the face had changed somehow in this day. A hint of a new purpose had crept into it, a purpose not possible for Dr. Fenneben to read.

But he did note the set of the head, the erect form and broad shoulders, and the easy swinging step as the boy went whistling away into the shadows of the night.

"A splendid animal, anyhow," the Dean thought. "Will the soul measure up to that princely body? And what can be the purport of this maudlin mouthing of old Bond Saxon? Bond is really a lovable man when he's sober; but he's vindictive and ugly when he's drunk. I can wait for developments. Whatever the boy's history may have been, like the courts, it's my business to hold every man innocent till he's proven guilty; to build up character, not to undermine and destroy it. And destruction begins in suspicion."

## CHAPTER VI. THE GAME

Truly ye come of The Blood; slower to bless than to ban;
Little used to lie down at the bidding of any man.
—KIPLING

BITTER weather followed the night of the storm. Biting winds beat all the autumn beauty from tree and shrub. Cold gray skies hung over a cold gray land, and a heavy snowfall and a penetrating chill seemed to destroy all hope for the Indian Summer that makes the Kansas Novembers glorious.

Dennie Saxon was the only girl of the party who was not affected by the storm at the Kickapoo Corral. Professor Burgess, who narrowly escaped pneumonia himself, and who disliked irregular class attendance, took comfort in the sight of Dennie. She was so fresh-checked and wholesome, and she went about her work promptly, forgetful of storm and rain and muddy ways.

"You seem immune from sickness, Miss Dennie," Burgess said one day as she was putting the library in order.

Under her little blue dusting cap, the sunny ripples of her hair framed a face glowing with health. She smiled up at him comfortably—a smile that played about the edges of his consciousness all that day.

"I've never been sick," she said. "It 's a good thing, too, for our house is a regular hospital this week. Little Bug Buler is the worst of all. He took cold on the night of the storm. That's why Victor Burleigh's out of school so much. He won't leave Bug."

Vincent Burgess despised the name of Burleigh now. While Vic's safe escort of Elinor Wream had increased his popularity with the students, Burgess honestly believed that old Bond Saxon's drunken speech hinted at some disgrace the big freshman would not long be able to conceal, and he resented the high place given to such a low grade of character. To a man like himself it was galling to look upon such a fellow as a rival. So, he tightened the rules and exacted the last mental farthing of Vic in the classroom. And Vic, easily understanding all this, because he was frankly and foolishly in love with the same girl whom Vincent Burgess seemed to claim, contrived in a thousand ways to make life a burden to the Harvard man. Of course, Burgess showed no mercy toward Vic for absence from the classroom while he was caring for little Bug, and the black marks multiplied against him.

Elinor Wream had been ill after the night of the storm. Vic had not seen her since the hour when he left her at Lloyd Fenneben's door. He knew he was a fool to think of her at all. He knew she must sometime be won by Burgess, and that she was born to gentle culture which his hard life had never known. Besides, he was poor. Not a pauper, but poor, and luxuries belonged naturally to a girl like Elinor. The storm of the holiday was a balmy zephyr compared to the storm that raged every day in him. For with all the hopelessness of things, he was in love. Poor fellow! The strength of his spirit was like the strength of his body—unbreakable.

He had no fear of pneumonia after the stormy night, for he was used to hard knocks. And he meant to go again by daylight and explore the rocky glen and hidden ways, and to find out, if possible, whose face it was that was behind that cavern wall, whose voice had whispered in his ear, and what loot was hidden there. For reasons of his own, he had mentioned this matter to nobody. But the cold, wet days, little Bug's illness, and the hard study to keep up his class standing, took all of his time. Especially, the study, that he might not be shut out of the great football game of the year on Thanksgiving day. Sunrise was stiff in its scholastic requirements, and conscientious to the last degree. The football team stood on mental ability and moral honor, no less than on scientific skill and muscular weight and cunning. Dr. Fenneben watched Burleigh carefully, for the boy seemed to be always on his heart. The Dean knew how to mix common sense and justice into his rulings, so the word was sent quietly from the head office—the suggestion of leniency in the matter of Burleigh's absence. Burleigh was good for it. It lay with his professors, of course, to grant or withhold scholarship ranking, but the Dean would be pleased to have all latitude given in Burleigh's case.

Bug was better now, and Vic was burning midnight oil in study, for the hours of practice for the game were doubled.

On the evening before Thanksgiving the coach called Vic aside.

"Everything is safe. Only one report not in, but it will be in tomorrow." the coach declared. "I asked Professor Burgess about your standing, and he says your grades are away above average. He's got to reckon up your absent marks, but that's easy. All the teachers understand about that. I guess Dean Funnybone fixed 'em. And now, Vic, the honor of Sunrise rests on you. If you fail us, we're lost. Can I count on you?"

The tiger light was behind the long black lashes under the heavy black brows, as Vic shut his white teeth tightly.

"Count on me!" he said, and turning, he left the coach abruptly.

"Hey, there, Burleigh, hold on a minute," Trench, the right guard, called, as Vic was striding up the steep south slope of the limestone ridge. "Say, wind a fellow, will you! You infernal, never-wear-out, human steam engine. I'm on to some things you ought to know. Even a lazy old scout like I am gets a crack at things once in a while."

"Well, get rid of it once in a while, if you really do know anything," Vic responded.

"Say, you're nervous. Coach says you spend too much time in your nursery; says you'd better get rid of that little kid."

"Tell the coach to go to the devil!" Vic spoke savagely.

"Say, Coach," Trench roared down from the hillslope, "Vic says for you to go to the devil."

"Wait till after tomorrow," the coach shouted back, "and I'll take you fellows along if you don't do your best."

"Now, that's settled, I'll tell you what I know," Trench drawled lazily. "First, Elinor Wream, what Dean Funnybone calls 'Norrie,' is heading the bunch that's going to shower us with roses tomorrow, if we win. And you know blamed well we'll win. They came in from

Kansas City on the limited, just now, the roses did. The shower's predicted for tomorrow P. M."

A sudden glow lighted Vic's stern face, and there was no savage gleam in his eyes now.

"Is Elinor well enough to come out tomorrow?"

He had been caught unawares. Trench stared at him deliberately.

"Say, Victor Burleigh." He spoke slowly. "Don't do it! DON'T DO IT! It will kill a man like you to get in love. Lord pity you! and"—more slowly still—"Lord pity the fool girl who can't see the solid gold in the rough old nugget you are."

"What's the rest of your news?" Vic asked.

"I gave the best first. Coach tells me ab-so-lute-lee, you are our only hope. The hope of Sunrise, tomorrow. You've got the beef, the wind, the speed, the head, and the will. Oh, you angel child!"

"The coach is clever," Vic said carelessly.

"Burleigh, here's the rub as well as the Rub-i-con. Dennie Saxon's wise, and she tells me—on the side; inside, not outside—that your absent marks on Burgess' map are going to cut you out at the last minute. Don't let Burgess do that, Vic, if you have to kill him. Couldn't we kidnap him and drop him into the whirlpool? Old Lagonda's interest is about due. Dennie just stood her ground today like a cherub, and asked the Hahvahd Univusity man right out about it. I don't know how she got the hint, only she's in all the offices and the library out of hours, you know, and when the slim one from Boston, yuh know, said as how he had to stand firm on the right, yuh know, old Dennie just says straight and flat, 'Professor Burgess, I'm ashamed of you.' Dennie's a brick. And do you know, Burgess, spite of his cussed thin hide, we've got to toughen for him out here in Kansas; spite of all that, HE LIKES DENNIE SAXON. The oracle hath orked, the sibyl hath sibbed. But say, Vic, if he does come down hard on you, what will you do?"

"Come down hard on him, and play anyhow."

The grim jaw and black frown left no doubt as to Vic's purpose.

Late November is idyllic in the Walnut Valley. Autumn's gold has all been burned in Nature's great crucible, refining the landscape to a wide range from frosted silver to richest Purple. Heliotrope and rose and amethyst blend with misty pink and dainty gray, and the faint, indefinable blue-green hue of the robin's egg, and outlined all in delicate black tracery of leafless boughs and darkened waterways. Every sunrise is a revelation of Infinite Beauty. Every midday, a shadowy soft picture of Peace. Every sunset a dream of Omnipotent Splendor.

On such a November Thanksgiving day, the great game of the season was played on the Sunrise football field, which all the Walnut Valley folks came forth to see.

By one o'clock Lagonda Ledge was deserted, save for old Bond Saxon, who sat on his veranda, watching the crowds stream by. At two o'clock the bleachers were packed, and the side lines were broad and black with a good-natured, jostling crowd. And every minute the numbers were increasing. Truly Sunrise had never before known such an auspicious day, such record-breaking gate receipts, nor such sure promise of success. The game was called for half-past two. It was three o'clock now and the line-up had not been formed. Even the gentle wrangle over details and eligibility could hardly have spun out so much time as seemed to the waiting throng to be uselessly wasted now. Evidently, something was wrong. The crowd grew impatient and demanded the cause. Out in the open, the two squads were warming up for the fray, while the officials hung fire in a group by the goal posts and talked threateningly.

"What's the matter?"

"When will the freight be in?"

"Merry Christmas!"

So the crowd shouted. The songs were worn out, the yell-leaders were exhausted, and the rooters were hoarse.

"Where's Vic Burleigh?" somebody called, and a chorus followed:

"Burleigh! Burly! Burlee! Come home! Come home! Come home!"

But Burleigh did not come.

"Maybe they are shutting him out," somebody else suggested, and the Sunrise bleachers took fire. Calls for Burleigh rent the air, roars and yells that threatened to turn this most auspicious college event into pandemonium, and the jolly company into a veritable mob.

Meantime, as the teams were leaving their quarters early in the afternoon, the coach said to Vic:

"Run up to Burgess and get your grades, Burleigh. It's a mere form, but it will save that gang of game-cocks from getting one over us."

In the rotunda Vic and Vincent met face to face, the country boy in his football suit and brown sweater, and the slender young college professor, with faultless tailoring and immaculate linen. Ten minutes before, Burgess had been in Dr. Fenneben's office, where Elinor Wream and a group of fair college girls were chattering excitedly.

"See these roses, Uncle Lloyd." Elinor was holding up a gorgeous bunch of American Beauties. "These go to Vic Burleigh when he gets behind the goal posts. Cost lots of my Uncle Lloyd's money, but we had to have them."

Small wonder that the very odor of roses was hateful to Burgess at that moment.

"May I speak to you a minute?" Vic said as the two men met in the rotunda.

Burgess halted in silence.

"The coach sent me after your statement of my standing. We've got a bunch of sticklers to fight today."

"I have turned in my report," Burgess responded coldly.

"So the coach said, all but mine. I'm late. May I have my report now?" Vic urged, trying to be composed.

"I have no further report for you." It was a cold-blooded thing to say, but Burgess, though filled with jealousy, was conscientious now in his belief that Burleigh was really a low grade fellow, deserving no leniency nor recognition.

"But you haven't given me any standing yet, the coach says." Vic's voice was dead calm.

"I have no standing to give you. You are below grade."

Vic's eyes blazed. "You dog!" was all he could say.

"Now, see here, Burleigh, there's no need to act any ruder than you can help." Burleigh did not move, nor did he take his yellow brown eyes from his instructor's face. "What have you to say further? I thought you were in a hurry." Burgess did not really mean a taunt in the last words.

"I have this to say." Victor Burleigh's voice had a menace in its depth and power. "You have done this infamous thing, not because I deserve it, but because you hate me on account of a girl—Elinor Wream."

"Stop!" Vincent Burgess commanded.

"I forbid you to mention her name. You, who come in here from some barren, poverty-stricken prairie home, where good breeding is unknown. You, to presume to think of such a girl as Dr. Fenneben's beautiful niece, whose reputation was barely saved by old Bond Saxon on the stormy night after the holiday. You, who are forced for some reason to care for an unknown child. You, whose true character will soon be fully known here—if this is what you have to say, you may go," he added with an imperious wave of the hand.

The meanness of anger is in its mastery. Burgess had meant only to discipline Burleigh, but it was too late for that now. The rotunda was very quiet. Everybody was down on the field waiting impatiently for the game to begin. Burgess was also impatient. There was a seat waiting for him beside Elinor Wream.

"I'm not quite ready to go"—Vic's fierce voice filled the rotunda—
"because you are going to write my credentials for this game, and
you'll do it quick, or beg for mercy."

"I refuse to consider a word you say." Burgess was furious now, and
the white face and burning eyes of his opponent were unbearable. "I
will not grant you any credentials, you low-born prize-fighter—"

A sudden grip of steel held him fast as Vic towered over him. The
softened light of the dome of the rotunda, where the Kansas motto,
*"Ad Astra per Aspera."* adorned the stained glass panes, had never
fallen on such a scene as this.

"See here, Burleigh, you'll repent this unwarranted attack," Burgess
cried, trying to free himself. "Brute force will win only among
brutes."

"That's the only place I expect to use it," Vic retorted, tightening his
grip. "No time for words now. The honor of Sunrise as well as my
honor is at stake, and it's my right to play in this game, because I
have broken no laws. I may have no culture except that of a prairie
claim; and I may be poor, and, therefore, presumptuous in daring to
mention Elinor Wream's name to you. But"—the brown eyes were a
blazing fire—"nobody can tell me that any man must rescue a girl
from me to save her reputation, nor that any dishonor belongs to me
because of little Bug Buler. Uncultured, as I am, I have the culture of
a courage that guards the helpless; and ill-bred, as I may be, I have a
gentleman's honor wherever a woman's need calls for my
protection."

Vic's face was ashy, for his anger matched his love, and both were
parallel to his wonderful physique and endurance. In his fury, the
temptation to throttle the man who had wronged him was gaining
the mastery.

"Vic, oh, Vic, they're waiting for you. Turn on! Don't hurt him, Vic."
Bug Buler's pleading little voice broke the momentary stillness.

Vic's hand fell nerveless, and Burgess staggered back.

"Was n't you dood to Vic? He would n't hurted you. He never hurted me." The innocent face and gentle words held a strange power over each passion-fired man before him.

Five minutes later, Vic Burleigh walked across the gridiron with full credentials for his place on the team.

The last man to enter the grounds was evidently a tramp, whose slouched hat half-concealed a dark bearded face.

As Vic Burleigh, with Bug clinging to his finger, hurried by the ticket window, the crippled student who sold tickets inside the little roofed box called out:

"Come, stay with me, Bug, till I can go in, too, and I'll buy you peanuts."

Bug studied a moment. Then with a comfortable little "Umph-humph," puffing out his pudgy cheeks with tightly tucked-in lips, he let go of Vic's finger and trotted over to the ticket box.

The boy let him inside and turned to the window to see the face of the tramp close to it. The man paid for a ticket, then, leaning forward, stared eagerly at the open money box. At the same time, the cripple caught sight of a revolver handle in a belt under the shabby coat. Trust a college boy for headwork. Instantly he seized little Bug by the shoulders and set him up on the shelf between the window and the money box. Bug's hair was a mop of soft ringlets, and his brown eyes and innocent baby face were appealing. The stranger stared hard at the child, and with a sort of frightened expression, shot through the gate and mingled with the crowd.

"Great protection for a cripple," the student thought, as he locked the money box. "How strong a baby's hand may be sometimes! Vic Burleigh's beef can win the game out there, but Bug has saved the day at this end of the line. That tramp seemed scared at the sight of him."

"Funny folks turns to dames," Bug observed.

"Yes, Buggie, the last one in before you came was a young woman with gray hair, and she had a big dog with her. They don't let in dogs, so he's waiting outside somewhere."

The last man who did not go in was Bond Saxon, who came late and found the gates deserted. But lying watchful in the open way, was a Great Dane dog. Old Bond hesitated. It was his lifetime fault to hesitate. Then he trotted back home. And, behold, a bottle of whisky was beside his doorstep. But to his credit for once, he resisted and smashed the bottle to bits on the stone step.

The day was made for such a game. There was no wind. The glare of the sun was tempered by a gray mist creeping up the afternoon skies. The air was crisp enough to prevent languor. The crowded bleachers were inspiring; the season was rounding out in a blaze of glory for Sunrise. The two teams were evenly matched, And the stern joy that warriors feel In foemen worthy of their steel, spurred each to its best efforts. It was a battle royal, with all the turns of strategy, and quickness, and straight physical weight, and sudden shifting of signals, fake plays, forward passes, line bucks, and splendid interference, flying tackles, speedy end runs, and magnificent defense of goals with lines of invincible strength and spirit.

With the kick-off the enemy's goal was endangered by a fumbled ball, and within three minutes Trench had torn a hole in the defense, through which the Sunrise team were sending Vic Burleigh for a touchdown. The bleachers went wild and the grandstand was almost shipwrecked in the noise.

"Burleigh! Burly! Burlee!" shrieked the yell-leader as Vic leaped over the goal line and the rooters roared:

The Sunrise hope!
And that's the dope!
Never quails!
Never fails!
Burleigh! Burly! Burlee!

A difficult kick from a sharp angle sent the ball through the air one inch wide of the goal post, and the bleachers counted five.

And then, came the forward swing again, the struggle for downs, the gain and loss of territory, until Trench, too heavy for speed, failed to break through the interference quickly enough to hold a swift little quarterback, who slipped around the end of the line, and, shaking off the tackles, swooped toward the Sunrise goal. The last defense was thrown headlong, and the field was wide open for the run; and the quarterback was running for the honor of his team, his school, his undying fame in the college world. Three yards to the goal line, and victory would be his. All Lagonda Ledge held its breath as Vic Burleigh tore through a tangle of tackles and sprang forward with long, space-eating bounds. He seemed to leap through ten feet of air, straight over the quarterback's head and land four feet from the goal with the quarterback in his grip, while a Sunrise halfback out beyond him was lying on the lost ball.

The bleachers now went entirely mad, for from the very edge of disaster, the tide of battle was turned into the enemy's territory. Before the Sunrise rooters had time to cease rejoicing, however, the invincible quarterback was away again, and with two guards and a center on top of Burleigh, now the plucky runner broke across the Sunrise line, and a minute later missed a pretty goal. And the opposing bleachers counted five.

The second half of the game was filled with a tense, fruitless strife. Five points to five points, and four minutes of time to play. The struggle had ceased to be a turning of tricks and test of speed. Henceforth, it was man against man, pound for pound. Suddenly, the opposing team braced itself and began a steady drive down the gridiron. With desperate energy, the Sunrise eleven fought for ground, giving way slowly, defending their goal like true Spartans, dying by inches, until only three yards of space were left on which to die. The rooters shrieked, and the girls sang of courage. Then a silence fell. Three yards, and the Sunrise team turned to a rock ledge as invincible as the limestone foundation of their beloved college halls. The center from which all strength radiated was Victor Burleigh. Against him the weight of the line-bucking plunged. If he wavered the line must crumble. The crowd hardly breathed, so tense was the strain. But he did not waver. The ball was lost and the last struggle of the day began. Two minutes more, the score tied, and only one chance was left.

Since the night of the storm, Vic had known little rest. His days had been spent in hard study, or continuous practice on the field; his nights in the sick room. And what was more destructive to strength than all of this was the newness and grief of a blind, overmastering adoration for the one girl of all the school impossible to him. The strain of this day's game, as the strain of all the preparation for it, had fallen upon him, and the half hour in the rotunda had sapped his energy beyond every other force. Love, loss, a reputation attacked, possible expulsion for assaulting a professor, injustice, anger—oh, it was more than a burden of wearied muscles and wracked nerves that he had to lift in these two minutes!

In a second's pause before the offense began, Vic, who never saw the bleachers, nor heard a sound when he was in the thick of the game, caught sight now of a great splash of glowing red color in the grandstand. In a dim way, like a dream of a dream, he thought of American Beauty roses of which something had been said once—so long ago, it seemed now. And in that moment, Elinor Wream's sweet face, with damp dark hair which the lamplight from Dr. Fenneben's door was illumining, and the softly spoken words, "I shall always remember you as one with whom I could never be afraid again"—all this came swiftly in an instant's vision, as the team caught its breath for the last onslaught.

"Victor, for victory. Lead out Burleigh," Trench cried to his mates, and the sweep of the field was on; and Lagonda Ledge and the whole Walnut Valley remembers that final charge yet. Steady, swift, invincible, it drove its strong foe down the white-crossed sod—so like a whirlwind, that the watching crowds gazed in bewilderment. Almost before they could comprehend the truth, the enemy's goal was just before the Sunrise warriors, and half a minute of time remained in which to play. One more line plunge with Burleigh holding the ball! A film came before his eyes. A sudden blankness of failure and despair seized him. In the grandstand, Elinor Wream stood clutching a pennant in both hands, her dark eyes luminous with proud hope. Amid all the yells and cheers, her sweet voice rang out:

"Victor, Victor! Don't forget the name your mother gave you!"

Vic neither saw nor heard. Yet in that moment, strength and pride and indomitable will power came sweeping back to him. One last plunge against this wall of defense upreared before him, and Burleigh, with half the enemy's eleven clinched to drag him back, had hurled himself across the goal line and lay half-conscious under a perfect shower of fragrant crimson roses, while the song of victory in swelling chorus pealed out on the November air. Half a minute later, Trench had kicked goal. The bleachers chanted eleven counts, the referee's whistle blew, and the game was done!

## SACRIFICE

The air for the wing of the sparrow,
The bush for the robin and wren,
But always the path that is narrow
And straight for the children of men.
—ALICE CARY

## CHAPTER VII. THE DAY OF RECKONING

Oh, it is excellent
To have a giant's strength, but tyrannous
To use it like a giant.
   —SHAKESPEARE

OF course, there came a day of reckoning for Victor Burleigh, now the idol of the Walnut Valley football fans, the pride of Lagonda Ledge, the hero of Sunrise. But the reckoning was not brought to him; he brought himself deliberately to it.

The jollification following the game threatened to wreck the chapel and crack the limestone ledge beneath it.

"Dust off your halo and wrap it up in cotton till next fall, Vic," Trench whispered in the closing minutes. "We've got to face the real thing now. We're civilians in citizens' clothes, amenable to law henceforth; not a lot of athletic brigands, privileged outlaws, whose glory dazzles all common sense. Quit bumping your head against the Kansas motto up in the dome, get your hob-nailers down on the sod, and trot off and tackle your Greek verbs awhile. And say, Vic, tackle yourself first and forget the pretty girl who covered you with roses down yonder five days ago. It was n't you, it was just the day's hero. She'd have decorated old Bond Saxon just the same if he had waddled across the last goal line then. You're a plug and she's a lady born, and as good as engaged to Burgess besides. I had that straight from Dennie Saxon, and you know Dennie's no gossip. They were far gone before they came West—the Wream-Burgess folk were— stiffen up, Burleigh. You look like a dead man."

"I was never more alive in my life." Vic's voice and eyes were alive enough.

"By heck! I believe it," Trench exclaimed. "Say, you got away with Burgess about the game. If you want the girl, go after her, too. But gently, Sweet Afton, go gently. Most girls want to do the pursuing themselves, I believe. I'll block the interference, if necessary, and you'll be the sought-after yet, not the seeking, dear child."

A circular stairway winds from the Sunrise chapel down the south turret to Dean Fenneben's study, intended originally as a sort of fire escape. Some enterprising janitor later fixed a spring lock on the upper door to this stairway (surprises had been sprung through this door upon the chapel stage by prankish students at inopportune moments), so that now it was only an exit, and was called by the students "the road to perdition," easy to descend but barred from retreat.

In the confusion following the chapel exercises Vic slipped into the south turret, and the lock clicked behind him as he hurried down "the road to perdition."

The door to Dean Fenneben's study was slightly open and Vic heard his own name spoken as he reached it. He hesitated, for a group of girls was surrounding Elinor Wream, discussing him. There was no escape. The upper door was locked, and he would rather have met that unknown villainous face in the dark cave than to face this group of pretty girls. So he waited.

"Oh, Elinor, you mercenary creature!"

"What if he is a bit crude?"

"I don't blame you. I'm daffy about Professor Burgess myself."

"He's got the grandest voice, Vic has!"

"I just adore Greek!"

"I think Vic is splendid!"

So the exclamations ran.

"Now, Norrie Wream, cross your heart, hope you may die, if big, handsome Victor Burleigh had his corners knocked off, and he was sandpapered down a little, and had money, wouldn't you feel a whole lot different about him, Norrie?"

"I certainly would. I couldn't help it."

Norrie's eyes were shining and her cheeks were pink as peach blossoms. To Vic she seemed exquisitely beautiful.

"But now?" somebody queried.

"Oh, now, she'll be sensible, and the Professor will take advantage of 'now.' He won't wait till it's too late. Great hat! there goes the bell."

And the girls scuttled away.

Vic came in and sat down by the window through which one may find an empire for the looking.

"Burgess was right," he said to himself.

"I'm not only ill-bred on the outside, I'm that way clear through. A disreputable eavesdropper! That's my size. But I didn't mean it. Fine excuse!" He frowned in disgust, and turned to the window.

The Thanksgiving weather was still blessing the Walnut Valley. Wide away beyond Lagonda Ledge rolled the free open prairies, swept by the free air of heaven under a beneficent sky.

As Vic gazed his stern face softened, and the bulldog look, that he had worn since the night of the storm, relaxed before some gentler mood. The brown eyes held a strange glow under the long black lashes, as if a new purpose were growing up in the soul behind them.

"No limit out there. It's a FREE LAND," he murmured. "There shall be no limit in here." Unconsciously he struck his breast with his fist. "There's freedom for such as I am somewhere."

"Hello, Burleigh, what can I do for you?" As Dr. Fenneben came into the study he recalled how awkwardly the same boy had filled the same chair only a few months before.

"I've come in to be sentenced," Vic replied.

"Well, plead your case first."

If ever a father-heart beat in a bachelor's breast, Lloyd Fenneben had such a heart.

"I want to settle about Thanksgiving Day," Vic said. "I had a moral right to play on the team in that game, but I had to get the legal right by force. Professor Burgess refused to permit me to play until I MADE him do it."

Fenneben's eyes were smiling. "Why didn't you knock him down and fight it out with him?"

"Because he's not in my class. When I fight I fight men. And, besides, I was in a hurry. If I'm expected to apologize to Professor Burgess or be expelled, I want to know it," Vic added, hotly.

He knew he would not apologize, and he wanted the sentence of expulsion to come quickly if it must come.

"We never expel boys from Sunrise. They have done it themselves sometimes. Nor do we ever exact an apology. They offer it themselves sometimes. In either case, the choice lies with the boy."

"What do you do with a fellow like me?" Vic looked curiously at the Dean.

"If a boy of your build wants to meet only men when he fights, we take it he is something of a man himself, and therefore worth too much for Sunrise to lose."

Oh! blessed power of the college man to lead the half-tamed boy into the stronger places of life; nor shove him to the dangerous ground where his feet must sink in the quicksand or the mire!

Vic sat looking thoughtfully at the man before him.

"Your confession here is all right. Your claim to a place on the team in Thursday's game was just." The simple fairness of Fenneben's words made their appeal, yet, it was so unlike what Vic had counted on he could hardly accept it as genuine.

"You have made a great name for yourself as an athlete. I paid for the roses. I know something of the degree of that greatness." Dr. Fenneben smiled genially. "You played a marvelous game and I am proud of you."

68

Vic did not look proud of himself just then, and Lloyd Fenneben knew it was one of life's crucial moments for the boy.

"The big letter S cut over the doorway out there stands for more than Sunrise, you remember I told you." Fenneben spoke earnestly. "It means also the strife which you have already met and must expect to meet all along the way. But, Burleigh"—Lloyd Fenneben stood up to his full height, an ideal of grace and power—"if you expect to make your way through college with your fists, come to me."

"You?" Vic's eyes widened.

"Yes, I'll meet you on any grounds. And if you ever try to coerce a professor here again, I'll meet you anyhow, and we'll have it out." Fenneben was stern now.

"I wouldn't want to scrap with you, Dr. Fenneben," Vic stammered.

"Why not?"

"I am too much of a gentleman for that."

"When I fight, I fight men. You are in my class," Fenneben quoted with a smile in his eyes, which faded away with the next words.

"You are right, Burleigh. A gentleman does n't want to use his strength like a beast to destroy. The only legitimate battle is when a man must fight with a man as he would fight with a beast, to save himself, or something dearer to him than himself, from beastly destruction. Get into the bigger game, my boy, where the strife is for larger scores, and add to a proud athletic record, the prouder record of self-control. The prairies have given you a noble heritage, but culture comes most from contact with cultured men. Don't take on airs because you have more red blood than our Harvard man. The influence of the great universities, directly or indirectly, on a life like yours is essential to your usefulness and power. You may educate your conscience to choose the right before the wrong, but, remember, an educated conscience does not always save a man from being a fool now and then. He needs an educated brain sometimes by which to save his soul. Meantime, settle with your conscience, if you owe it anything. It is a troublesome creditor. I'll leave you now to square yourself with that fellow you must live with every day—Victor Burleigh. We'll drop everything else henceforth and face toward tomorrow, not yesterday."

Lloyd Fenneben grasped the boy's hand in a firm, assuring grip and left him.

"If Sunrise means Strife, I'll face it," Vic said to himself. "As to money, I have only my two hands and that old mortgaged quadrangle of prairie sod out West. But if culture like Fenneben's might win Elinor Wream, God help me to win it."

Up in the library a week later Professor Burgess came in while Dennie Saxon was putting the books in order. Burgess was often to be found where Dennie was, but Burgess himself had not noted it, and nobody else knew it, except Trench. Trench was a lazy fellow, who always lived in the middle of his pasture, where the feeding was good. That gave him time to study mankind as it worried about the outer edges.

"Don't you get tired sometimes, Miss Dennie?" the Professor asked. He was not happy himself for many reasons, and two of them were Elinor and Vic, who separately, and differently, seemed to wear out his energy. Dennie Saxon never wore on anybody's nerves.

"Yes, I do, often," Dennie answered.

"Why do you do this?" he queried.

"To get my college education." Dennie smiled, hopefully. "I like the nice things and nice ways of life. So I'm working for them."

"Elinor has all these without working for them," Vincent thought.

Then for no reason at all his mind leaped to Dennie's father and his own vow on the stormy night in October.

"What would you do if your father were taken from you, Miss Dennie?" he asked.

"I've always had to depend on myself somewhat. I would keep on, I suppose." Dennie looked up bravely. Her father was her joy and her shame.

Well, what had Burgess expected? That she would depend on him? He was in love with Elinor Wream. Why should he feel disappointed? And why should his eye follow the soft little ripples of her sunny hair, giving a pretty outline to her face and neck.

"Could you really take care of yourself? He was talking at random.

"I might do like that woman out at Pigeon Place." Burgess did n't catch the pathos in Dennie's tone. He was only a man.

"How's that?" he asked.

"Oh, live alone and keep a big dog, and sell chickens. That's what Mrs. Marian does. By the way, she looks just a little bit like you."

"Thank you!"

"She was at the game on Thanksgiving Day, strange to say, for she seldom leaves home. Did you see a pretty white-haired woman, right south of where we were?"

"Is that how I look? No, I didn't see her. I was n't at the game."

"You weren't? Why not? You missed a wonderful thing."

And Burgess told her the whole story from his viewpoint, of course. What he was too proud to mention to Dr. Fenneben or Elinor he spoke of freely to Dennie, and he felt as if the weight of the limestone ledge was lifted from him with the telling.

"Don't you think the young ruffian was pretty hard on me?" he asked.

"No, I don't," Dennie said, frankly. "I think you were pretty hard on him."

A sudden resolve seized Burgess. He came around to Dennie's side of the table.

"Miss Dennie, I want to tell you something, unimportant in itself, but better shared than kept. On the night of our picnic in October your father, who was not quite himself—"

"Yes, I understand," Dennie said, with downcast eyes.

"Pardon me, Dennie, I would not hurt your feelings." His voice was very gentle, and Dennie looked up gratefully. "On that night your father made me promise—made me hold up my hand and swear— I'm easily forced, you will think—to look after you if he were taken away. I did it to pacify him, not to ever embarrass you. He also told me enough about young Burleigh to make me wish, in the office of protector, to warn you."

"Was my father quite himself then?" Dennie asked.

"Not quite," Burgess replied.

"Listen to him some day when he is. He is another man then. But," she added, "I know you mean well."

In spite of her courage her eyes were full of tears, and for the first time in his sheltered pleasant life the real spirit of sympathy woke in the soul of Vincent Burgess.

"You are a brave, good girl, Dennie. If I can ever serve you in any way, it will be a privilege to me to do it."

Ten minutes after they had left the library Trench, who had been stationary in the north alcove, slowly came to life. He had been posing as a statue, Winged Victory with a head on, he declared afterward to Vic Burleigh, to whom he told the whole story.

"Let me sing my swan song," he declared. "Then me for Lagonda's whirlpool. I'm not fit to live in a decent community, a blithering idiot and rascally villain, who lies in wait to hear and see like a fool. I thought Dennie knew I was there and would be in to dust me out in a minute. And when it was too late I turned to a pillar of salt and waited. But I believe I'll change my mind, after all. I'll live; and if Professor Burgess, A.B. of Cambridge-by-the-bean-patch, dares to make love to Dennie Saxon—on the side—he'll go head foremost into the whirlpool to feed Lagonda's rapacious spirit. I've said it."

## CHAPTER VIII. LOSS, OR GAIN?

We cannot make bargains for blisses,
　　Nor catch them like fishes in nets,
And sometimes the thing our life misses
　　Helps more than the thing which it gets.
　　　　　—CARY

ELINOR WREAM spent the holidays in the East and was two weeks late in entering school again. Then her Uncle Lloyd tightened the rules, exacting full measure for lost time, until she bewailed to her girl friends that she had no opportunity even to make fudge or wash her hair.

"Were you sorry to come back, then, Norrie?" her uncle asked one evening when they were alone in their library, and Elinor was lamenting her hard lot.

"No, I want to be with you, Uncle Lloyd."

She was sitting on the arm of his morris chair, softly stroking his heavy hair away from his forehead.

"Looks like it, the way you hurried back," Dr. Fenneben said, smiling.

"But Uncle Joshua is n't well, although, to be honest, he didn't seem a bit anxious to have me stay. He's so wrapped up in Sanscrit he has no time to live in the present. Why didn't he ever marry?"

"You have just said why," her uncle answered her.

"Why did n't you ever marry. Were you ever in love?"

The library lamp cast only a shaded light over Lloyd Fenneben lounging comfortably in his chair. To a woman's eye he would have seemed the picture of an ideal husband.

"Yes, I was in love once. I did n't marry because—because—I didn't."

"How romantic! Was it unrequited, or money, or what?" Norrie asked, eagerly.

"Or what," he answered, and her finer sense made her change the subject.

"Say, Uncle Lloyd, Uncle Joshua says he wants me to marry."

"What's he up to now? Tell me about it."

Norrie was charming tonight in a dainty red evening gown that set off her pretty face, crowned with beautiful dark hair. Somehow the sight of her made deeper the void in Fenneben's life—since that love affair of his own long ago.

"Well," Norrie went on, "Uncle says I'm to marry rich, because my papa expected me to. He said papa had money which was mamma's and he used it for college endowments, because the Wreams love colleges best, and that it was his wish, and it's Uncle Joshua's too, that I should marry well. I knew I came honestly by my love of spending. I inherited it from my mother. Aren't the Wreams all funny men to just see nothing in money, but a cap and gown and a Master's Degree? But you are a human being, Uncle Lloyd. You wouldn't leave a daughter dependent on her uncles and use her money to endow colleges, would you?" The white arm stole round his neck affectionately, as Elinor added softly, "I'm going to tell you something else. Uncle Joshua wants me to marry Professor Burgess."

"Do you want to marry him?" Fenneben asked.

"He hasn't asked me to yet. But he is such a gentleman and he has a fortune in his own name, or in trust, or something like that. It would please the Cambridge folks, and Uncle Joshua expects me to consent, and I've never disobeyed uncle's wishes, so I couldn't refuse now. And, well, if he'll wait till I'm ready, I guess it will suit me."

"He'll wait all right, if he wants you, Norrie. He must wait until you graduate," the Dean declared.

"Oh, yes; a Wream without a college diploma is like a ship without a compass, a mere derelict on life's sea. I'm in no hurry anyhow," and she began to talk of other things.

In the months that followed Trench had no need to watch Professor Burgess in his relation to Dennie Saxon, for Burgess had no thought of her other than of kindly sympathy. That is, Burgess thought he had no thought. He knew he was in love with Elinor, knew that back in Cambridge before he was graduated from the university. He had been told that Elinor liked luxurious living, and he had money—he had told Fenneben as much in their first interview. Everything seemed to be settled now, for Joshua Wream had written Burgess the kind of letter only a very old man, and an abstract scholar, and a bachelor would ever write, telling all that he had said to Norrie. He made it obligatory that Fenneben should first give his sanction to the union. He requested also that Burgess would never mention this letter to his dear young niece, and he expressly stipulated that Norrie should graduate at Sunrise first. He ended with an old man's blessing and with the assurance that with Elinor safely provided for his conscience (why his conscience?) would be at rest, and he could die in peace. So there was smooth sailing at Sunrise for many months. Elinor was always charming, and Dr. Fenneben seemed oblivious to the situation, least of all to putting up any objection, which, according to brother Joshua, would have blocked the game of love. There was time now for profound research, the study of types, seclusion, and the advantage of geographical breath which had brought the Professor to Kansas, and which he heeded less and less with the passing days. For he found himself more and more living in the lives of the students. He had been ashamed, once, of having been Dennie Saxon's escort; and he never knew when she came to be the one person in Lagonda Ledge to whom he turned for confidence and aid in many things.

Meanwhile the big boy from the western claim was as surely going up the rounds of culture as the Professor was coming down to the common needs of common minds, and both were unconscious then that back of each was Dr. Fenneben, "dear old Funnybone" to the student body, playing each man for his king row in the great game of life fought out in Sunrise-by-the-Walnut.

Toward Elinor, Victor Burleigh seemed utterly indifferent. Even Lloyd Fenneben, who had caught an insight into things on the night of the October storm, and had begun to read that new line in the boy's face, failed to grasp what lay back of those innocent-looking, wide-open eyes, whose tiger-golden gleam showed but rarely now. Vic was easily the most popular fellow in his class, and the year at Sunrise had worked a marvelous change in him.

"You are a darned smooth citizen," Trench drawled, as he and Burleigh stood in the shade by the campus gate on the closing day of their freshman year.

A group of girls had been bidding the two good-bye for the summer. As Elinor Wream, who was the last one of the company, offered her hand to Vic there was a look of expectancy in her glance which found no response in his own eyes. As he turned away with indifferent courtesy to Trench, the big right guard stared hard at him.

"You are a—well, any kind of a smooth citizen, I say," he repeated.

"What's troubling your liver now?" Vic asked.

Trench did not heed the question, but said, slowly: "And-the-big-noble-    hearted-young-fellow-walked-in-and-out-beside-how-the-touch-of-her-hand-    thrilled-his-every-pulse-beat,-and-how-her-smile-was-the-light-of-his-    soul.    And-he-grew-handsomer-and-more-beloved-with-the-passing-manhood—"

A sudden clutch on Trench's arm, the blaze of the old-time fury in burning eyes, as Vic's hoarse voice cried:

"For God's sake, Trench, get out of my sight!"

"I will," drawled Trench. "The only friend you ever had. I'll carry my troubles up to Big Chief Funnybone. Like as not he'll sentence me to tumble you through the chapel door of the south turret down the 'road to perdition.' No use though, you go that road every day. Better treat me right and tell me all your troubles. If there is any cool handle to take hold of Gehanna by next to Funnybone, I'm the one fellow in Sunrise to grab onto it."

But Vic was out of hearing.

And the days of a long, hot Kansas summer, a glorious autumn, and a short, nippy winter swung by in their appointed seasons. And now the springtime was unrolling in dainty beauty of tender green leaf, and growing grass, and warm, sweet air, and trill of song bird. College students philosophize little in the springtime of their sophomore year. Having learned all that books can teach, and a little more, they seek other pastime. Nobody in Sunrise except Dr. Fenneben took the time to remember how stiff and ungenial Professor Burgess was when he first came West; nor what an awkward gosling Victor Burleigh was the day he entered Sunrise; nor that once it could have seemed just a little odd to invite Dennie Saxon, a poor student, daughter of a half-reformed drunkard, to the class parties; nor that even Elinor Wream, "Norrie the beloved," was not supposed to be engaged to Vincent Burgess. Supposed! And that, when her senior year was well along, the engagement would be openly spoken of as now in her sophomore year, it was quietly accepted, even if Professor Burgess was often Dennie Saxon's escort. That was because he was such a gentleman. Nor that with all these changes Trench had remained the same old lazy Trench, the comfortable idol of the girls, for he was right guard to all of them, and cared for none. And they never knew till afterward that for all the four years he was faithful to a little sweetheart out in the sandy Cimarron River country, to whom he took back clean hands and a pure heart, when he went home after four years of college life.

None of these things were noted especially, save by Dr. Lloyd Fenneben, and he wasn't a sophomore nor a professor in love with a pretty girl; a professor learning for the first time that sympathy has also its culture value, as well as perfectly translated Horace, and that the growth of a human soul means something as beautiful as the growth of a complete conjugation on an old Greek stem from an older Greek root. Fenneben had learned all this while he was chasing about the Kansas prairies with a college in his vest pocket.

There were some unchanged things, however, which Fenneben only guessed at. Victor Burleigh had never apologized to Professor Burgess for his rude attack, unless a certain strained dignified courtesy be the mark of a tacit apology. And Burgess could give only cold recognition to the big fellow who had choked him into submission and had gone unpunished by the college authorities.

Between these two Fenneben guessed there was no change. But he did not grieve deeply. There must be a personal phase in this grudge that no third person could handle. It might be a girl—but the face of the returns indicated otherwise. Meanwhile the college was doing its perfect work for Burleigh, whose strength of mind, and self-control, and growing graciousness of manner betokened the splendid manhood that should rest on this foundation. While the spirit of the prairie sod, the benediction of the broad-sweeping air of heaven, and the sturdy, wholesome life of the sons and daughters of freedom-loving, broad-spirited men and women—all were giving to Vincent Burgess a new happiness in his work unlike any pleasure he had ever known before.

Little Bug Buler, now four years of age, had changed least of all among changing things about Lagonda Ledge. A sweet-faced, quaint little fellow he was, with big appealing eyes, a baby lisp to his words, and innocent ways. He was a sturdy, pudgy, self-reliant youngster, however, who took long rambles alone and turned up safe at the right moment. All Lagonda Ledge petted him, even to Burgess, who never forgot the day in the rotunda when Bug's pitying voice had broken Burleigh's grip on his neck.

Bond Saxon had not changed, nor the white-haired woman of Pigeon Place—nor the reputation of the ravines and rocky coverts for hiding law breakers across the Walnut River. And Fenneben noted often the slender blue smoke rising where nobody had a house.

It was an April day in the Walnut Valley, with all the freshness of the earth just washed and perfumed by April showers. The sunshine was pale gold. There was a gray-green filmy light from budding trees, and the old-time miracle of the grass was wrought out once more before the eyes of men. The orchards along the Walnut were faintly pink, and the eggs in the robin's nest, the south winds purring through the wooded spaces, the odor of far-plowed furrows on the prairie farms, all gave assurance of the year's gladdest days. From the Sunrise ledge the beauty of the landscape was exquisite.

There was no haze overhanging the earth now, and the Walnut Valley was a picture beyond a Master's dream. Victor Burleigh sat on the top of the flight of steps leading from the lower campus, looking lazily out with dreamy eyes on all that the earth had to give on this sweet April afternoon.

Presently Elinor Wream came around the north angle of the building, hesitated a little, then walked straight to the steps.

"Good afternoon, Victor," she said.

Burleigh looked up, glad then of his months of discipline and self-control. A sight good for anybody on a day like this was this college girl with beautiful dark hair and laughing dark eyes, a satiny pink and white complexion, and a slender form, clad just now in dainty pink gingham with faint little edgings of white and pale green, all stylishly put together to reveal rounded arms, and white neck, and dimpled chin.

"Hello, Elinor," Vic said, calmly, making room for her on the stone steps. "Take a seat."

Elinor sat down beside him, throwing her hat on the ground.

"Whither away?" Vic asked.

"I'll tell you presently. I want to get over my stage fright first."

"All right, look at this view. I'll give it to you if you like it." Vic had turned to the west again and was looking away toward the dreamy prairies beyond the valley.

Elinor recalled the September day when the bull snake lay sunning itself on this very stone. How shy and awkward he seemed then, with only a deep sweet voice to attract favorable attention. And now, big, and graceful, and handsome, and reserved—any girl might be proud to have his regard. Of course, for herself, there was Vincent Burgess in the pleasant inevitable sometime. She gave little thought to that. She was living in the present. And in the wooing spirit of the April afternoon Elinor was glad to sit here beside Victor Burleigh.

"What time next month do we have the big baseball game?" she asked. "The game that is to make Sunrise the champion college in Kansas, and you our college champion?" Vic's lips suddenly grew gray.

"Friday, the thirteenth—auspicious date!" he answered. "But I may not play in it. I might fail."

"Oh, we must win this game, anyhow, and you never do fail. Don't forget the name your mother gave you. Do you remember when you told me that?"

"A couple of thousand years ago, wasn't it?" Vic asked, smiling down on her. "If I don't play Sunrise needn't fail, even for Friday, the thirteenth."

"But it will fail without you. You pulled us to victory a year ago at the Thanksgiving game, and last fall the Sunrise goal line wasn't crossed the whole season with 'Burleigh! Burly! Burlee!' for a slogan. We must win this year. Then it will be a complete championship: football, basket-ball, and baseball. We won't do it though unless we have 'Burleigh at the bat'."

A shadow crossed his face and he looked away to where a tiny film of blue smoke was rising above the rough ledges beyond the river.

"I'm getting over my stage fright now," Elinor said, the pink deepening on her fair cheek, "and I'll tell you what I want."

"Command me!" he said, gallantly.

"Well, it's awful, and the girls are too mean to live. But they are getting even with me, they say, for something I did last fall."

"All right." Vic was waiting, graciously.

"A lot of us have broken some of the rules of the Sorority and it's decreed that I must go over the route we came home by on the night of the storm down in the Kickapoo Corral. They are having a 'spread' down there at five o'clock and we are to get there in time for it, going by the west side of the river, and they'll bring us home.

They said I should ask you to go with me, and if you would n't go for me to ask Mr. Trench to go. They are too silly for anything."

"Trench was executed for manslaughter at two forty-five today. It's three o'clock now. Let's go." He lifted her to her feet and stooped to pick up her hat.

"Do you really mind going with me, Victor?" Elinor asked.

"Do I mind? I've been waiting two years for you to ask me to go." His voice was very deep and there was a soft light in his brown eyes.

Elinor's pulse beat felt a thrill. A sudden sense of the sweetness of the day and of a joy unlike any other joy of her life possessed her.

Down on the bridge they stopped to watch the sunlit waters of the Walnut rippling below them.

"Are we the same two who crept up on this bridge, wet, and muddy and tired, and scared one stormy October night eighteen months ago?" Elinor asked.

"I've had no reincarnation that I know of," Vic replied.

"I have," Elinor declared, and Vic thought of Burgess.

Up the narrow hidden glen they made their way, clambering about broken ledges, crossing and recrossing the little stream, hugging the dry footing under overhanging rock shelves, laughing at missteps and rejoicing in the springtime joy, until they came suddenly upon a grassy open space, cliff-walled and hidden, even from the rest of the glen. At the farther end was the low doorway-like entrance to the cave. The song-birds were twittering in the trees above them, the waters of the little stream gurgled at their feet, the woodsy odor of growing things was in the air, and all the little glen was restful and quiet.

"Isn't it beautiful and romantic—and everything nice?" Elinor cried. "I don't mind this sentence to hard service. It is worth it. Do you mind the loss of time, Victor?"

"I counted it gain to be here with you, even in the storm and terror. How can this be loss?" he answered her. His voice was low and musical.

Elinor looked up quickly. And quickly as the thing had come to Victor Burleigh on the west bluff above the old Kickapoo Corral two Octobers ago, so to Elinor Wream came the vision of what the love of such a man would be to the woman who could win it.

"Do you really mean it, Victor? Was n't I a lump of lead? A dead weight to your strength that night? You have never once spoken of it."

She looked up with shining eyes and put out her hand. What could he do but keep it in his own for a moment, firm-held, as something he would keep forever.

"I have never once forgotten it," he murmured.

The cave by daylight was as the lightning had shown it, a big chamber, rock-walled, rock-floored, rock-roofed, in the side of the bluff, but little below the level of the ground and easy of entrance. It was cool and damp, but, with the daylight through the doorway, it was merely shadowy inside. In the farther wall yawned the ragged opening to the black spaces leading off underground. Through this opening these two had crept once, feeling that behind the wall somebody was crouching with evil intent. They peered through the opening now, trying to see the miraculous way by which they had come into the cave from the rear. But they stared only into blackness and caught the breath of the damp underground air with a faint odor of wood smoke somewhere.

"Elinor, it's a good thing we came through here in the night. It would have been maddening to be forced in here by daylight. We must have slipped down through a hole somewhere in our stumbles and hit a passage leading out of here only to the river, a sort of fire escape by way of the waters. You remember we couldn't get anywhere on the back track, except to the cliff above the Walnut. It's all very fine if the escaper gets out of the river before he reaches Lagonda's whirlpool."

He was leaning far through the opening in the wall, gazing into the darkness and seeing nothing.

"Somewhere back in there, while I was pawing around that night, I found something up in a chink that felt like the odd-shaped little silver pitcher my mother had once—an old family heirloom, lost or stolen some time ago. I came back and hunted for it later, but it was winter time and cold as the grave outside and darker in here, and I couldn't find anything, so I concluded maybe I was mistaken altogether about its being like that old pitcher of ours. It was a bad night for 'seein' things'; it might have been for 'feelin' things' as well. There's nothing here but damp air and darkness."

And even while he was speaking close beside the wall, so near that a hand could have reached him, a man was crouching; the same man whose cruel eyes had stared through the bushes at Lloyd Fenneben as he sat by the river before Pigeon Place; the same man whose eyes had leered at Vic Burleigh in this same place eighteen months before; the same man whom little Bug Buler's innocent face had startled as he was about to seize the money box at the gateway to the Sunrise football field; and this same man was crouching now to spring at Vic Burleigh's throat in the darkness.

"It's a good thing a fellow has a guardian angel once in a while," Vic said, as he hastily withdrew his head and shoulders. "We get pretty close to the edge of things sometimes and never know how near we are to destruction."

"We were pretty close that night," Elinor replied.

"Shall we rest here a little while, or do your savage sorority sisters require you to do time in so many minutes?" Vic asked, as they left the cave and came again into the sunlight, and all the sweetness of the April woodland, and the rugged beauty of the glen.

"I'm glad to rest," Elinor said, dropping down on a stone. Her cheeks were blooming from the exercise of the tramp, and her pretty hair was in disorder.

Far away from the west prairie came the faint note of a child's voice in song.

"Victor," Elinor said, as they listened, "do you know that the Sunrise girls envy Bug Buler? They say you would have more time for the girls if it wasn't for him. What you spend for him you could spend on light refreshments for them, don't you see?"

"I know I'm a stingy cuss," Vic said, carelessly, but a deeper red touched his cheek.

"You know you are not," Elinor insisted, "and I've always thought it was a beautiful thing for a big grown man like you to care for a little orphan boy. All the girls think so, too."

Burleigh looked down at her gratefully.

"I thought once—in fact, I was told once—that my care for him was sufficient reason why I should let all the girls alone, most of all why I should not think of Elinor Wream."

"How strange!" Elinor's face had a womanly expression. "I've never had a little child to love me. I've been brought up with only AEneas's small son Ascanius, and other classical children, on Uncle Joshua's Dead Language book shelves. I feel sometimes as if I'd been robbed."

"You? I didn't know you had ever wanted anything you did n't get."

Victor had thought all things were due to her and came as duly. The womanly look on her face now was a revelation to him. But then he had not dared to study her face for months, and he did not yet realize what life in Dr. Fenneben's home must mean to her character-building.

"I'll tell you some time about something I ought to have had, a sacrifice I was forced to make; but not now, Tell me about Bug."

There was no bitterness in Elinor's tone, yet the idea of her having the capacity to endure gave her a newer charm to the man beside her.

"I have never known whose child Bug is," he began. "The way in which he came to me is full of terrible memories, and it all happened on the blackest day of my life—the hard life of a lonely boy on a

Kansas claim. That's why I never speak of it and try always to forget it. I found him by mere accident, helpless and in awful danger. He was about two years old then and all he could say was 'bad man' and his name, 'Bug Buler.' I've wondered if Bug is his name, or if he could not speak his real name plainly then."

Burleigh paused, and a sense of Elinor's interest brought a thrill of joy to him.

"Where was he?" she asked.

Vic slowly unfastened his cuff and slipped his coat sleeve up to his elbow.

"Do you remember that scar?" he asked. "It is not the only one I have. I fought with death for that baby boy and I shall always carry the scars of that day. Bug was alone in a lonely little deserted dugout. Somebody had left him there to perish. He was on a low chair, the only furniture in the room, and on the earth floor between him and me were five of the ugliest rattlesnakes that ever coiled for a deadly blow. Little Bug held out his arms to me, and I'll never forget his baby face—and—I killed them all and carried him away. It was a dangerous, hard job, but the boy I saved has been the blessing of my life ever since. I could not have endured the days that followed without his need for care and his love and innocence. He's kept me good, Elinor. When I got back home with him my mother, who had been very sick, was dead, and our house had been robbed of every valuable by some thief—a wayside tragedy of western Kansas. That was the day the pitcher was stolen. A note was left warning me not to follow nor try to find out who had done the stealing, but I thought I knew anyhow. That's why I killed that bull snake the first day I came to Sunrise and that's why I must have looked like a bulldog to you, soft-sheltered Cambridge folks. Life has been mostly a fist fight for me, but Dr. Fenneben has taught me that there are other powers beside physical strength. That the knock-down game doesn't bring the real victory always. I hope I've learned a little here."

A little! Could this be the big awkward freshman of a September day gone by? Then college culture is surely worth the cost.

Elinor leaned forward, eagerly.

"Tell me about your father," she said.

"My father lost his life because he dared to tell the truth," Victor replied.

"Oh, glorious!" Elinor cried, earnestly.

"I have always loved my father's memory for his courage," Victor continued. "He was a believer in law enforcement and he was a terror to the bootleggers who carried whisky into our settlement. A man named Gresh was notorious for selling whisky to the claim holders. He gave it, Elinor, gave it, to a boy, a widow's son, made him drunk, robbed him, and left him to freeze to death in a blizzard. The boy lived long enough to tell my father who did it, and it was his testimony that helped to convict Gresh and start him to the penitentiary. He escaped from the sheriff on the way—and, so far as I know, there's one bad man still at large, a fugitive before the law. Whisky is the devil's own best tool, whether a man drinks it himself or gets other people to drink it."

"That's a bad name," Elinor said. "My grandfather adopted a boy named Gresh, who turned out bad. I think he was killed in a saloon row in Chicago. Did this Gresh ever trouble you again?"

Burleigh's face was grim as he answered:

"My father was waylaid and murdered with a club by this man. He escaped afterward into Indian Territory. He left his own name, Gresh, scrawled on a piece of paper pinned to my father's coat to show whose revenge was worked out. He was a volcano of human hate—that man Gresh. After my father's name was written—'The same club for every Burleigh who ever crosses my path.' I expect to cross his path some day, and if I ever lay my eyes on that fiend it will go hard with one of us." The yellow glow burned again in Victor Burleigh's eyes and his fists clinched involuntarily. They were silent a while, until the sweetness of the day and the joy of being together wooed them to happier thoughts. Then Elinor remembered her disordered hair and, throwing aside her hat, she deftly put it into place.

"Am I presentable for the supper at the Kickapoo Corral?" she asked, as she picked up her hat again.

"You suit me," Burleigh replied. "What are the Kickapoo requirements?"

"That Victor Burleigh shall be satisfied," she answered, roguishly. "Really, that's right. Four girls offered to substitute for me in this penitential pilgrimage and write some long translations for me beside."

"Four, individually or collectively?" he asked.

"Either way," she answered.

"Why did n't you let them do it?

"Which way?"          •

"Either way," he replied.

"Would you rather have had the four either way, than me?" she questioned, with pretty vanity.

"Much rather." His voice was stern.

"Why?" She was stung by the answer.

The glen was all a dreamy gray-green ruggedness of shelving rock with mossy crevices and ferny nooks. The sunlight filtering through the young leaves fell about them in a shadow-flecked softness. There was a crooning song of some bird on its nest, the murmur of waters rippling down the stony shallows, and a beautiful girl in a dainty pink dress with her fingers just touching her fluffy masses of hair.

"Why?"

With the question Elinor looked up and saw why. Saw in Victor Burleigh's golden-brown eyes a look she had never read in eyes before; saw the whole face, the rugged, manly face lighted with a man's overmastering love. And the joy of it thrilled her soul.

"Do you know why?"

He leaned toward her ever so little. And Elinor Wream, forgetful of the Wream family rank, forgetful of her tacit consent to Uncle Joshua's wishes, forgetful of Vincent Burgess and his heritage of culture, beautiful Elinor Wream, with her starry eyes, and cheeks of peach-blossom pink, put out her hands to Victor Burleigh, who took them eagerly.

"Let me hold them a minute," he said, softly. "There are sixty years to remember, but only one hour like this."

Then, forgetful of the world and the demands of the world, keeping her hands in his, he bent and kissed her, as from the foundation of the world it was his right to do. And Love's Young Dream, not bought with pain, as mother love is bought, nor wrought out with prayer and sacrificial service, as love for all humanity is won, came again on this April day to the little, rock-sheltered glen beside the bright waters of the Walnut, and briefly there rebuilt in rainbow hues the old, old paradise of joy for these two alone.

And into the new Eden came the new serpent also for to destroy. Before Elinor and Victor was the sunlit valley. Behind them was the cave's mouth with its shadowy gloom deepening back to dense darkness. And creeping stealthily through that blackness, like a serpent warming its venom and writhing slowly toward the light, a human form was slowly, stealthily crawling outward, with head upreared and cruel eyes alert. The brutal face was void of pity, as if the conscience behind it had long been bound and gagged to human sympathy.

While Burleigh was speaking the caveman had reached the doorway and reared up just beside it in the shadow. Clutching a brutal-looking club in his hairy, rough hand, he stood listening to the story of the murder that had left Victor fatherless. The face of the listener made clear the need for guardian angels. One leap, one blow, and Victor Burleigh would carry only one more scar to his grave.

Suddenly a faint piping voice floated in upon the glen:

> Little childwen pwessing near
>   To the feet of Thwist, the Ting,
> Have you neiver doubt nor fear
>   Or some twibute do you bwing?

And Bug Buler, flushed and splashed, and generally muddy and happy, came around the fallen ledges and debauched into the grassy sunshiny space before the cavern. Only a tiny, tumbled-up, joyous child, with no power in his pudgy little arm; and Victor Burleigh, tall, muscular and agile. Against this man of tremendous strength the caveman's club was lifted. But with the sound of the child's voice and the sight of the innocent face the club fell harmless. A look of fright, deepening to a maniac's terror, seized the creature, and noiselessly and swiftly as a serpent would escape he crawled back into the darkness and burrowed deep from the eyes of men. So strength that day was ruled by weakness.

"I ist followed you, Vic," Bug said, clutching Vic's hand.

"This is n't a safe place to come, Bug. You must n't follow me here."

"Nen you must n't go into is n't safe places, so I won't follow. Little folks don't know," Bug said, with cunning gravity.

"He is right," Elinor said. "I think we'd better leave now."

They knew that henceforth this spot would be holy ground for them, but they did not dare to think further than that. They only wished that the moments would stay, that the sun would loiter slowly down the afternoon sky.

"I know a way out," Bug declared. Turn, "I'll show you."

Then, with a child's sense of direction, he led away from the cave out to where the deep ravine headed in a rough mass of broken rock.

"Tlimb up that and you're out," Bug declared.

They climbed up to the high level prairie that sweeps westward from the Walnut bluffs.

"Doodby, folks. I want to Botany wiv urn over there. I turn wiv Limpy out here."

Bug pointed to a group of students wandering about in search of dogtooth violets and other botanical plunder from Nature's springtime treasury. Among the group was Bug's chum, the crippled student.

"Well, stay with them this time, you little wandering Jew," Vic admonished, nor dreamed how his guardian angel had come to him this day in the guise of this same little wanderer.

When Victor and Elinor had come at last to the west bluff above the Walnut River, the late afternoon was already casting long shadows across the grassy level of the old Kickapoo Corral. And again the camp fires were glowing where a Sorority "spread" was merrily in the making.

They must go down soon and join in the hilarity. But a golden half hour yet hung in the west—and the going down meant the going back to all that had been.

"Look at the foam on the whirlpool, Elinor. See how deliberately it swings upstream. Isn't that a most deceiving bit of treachery?" Vic said as he watched the river.

Elinor looked thoughtfully at the slow-moving water.

"I cannot endure deceit," she said at last. "I like honesty in everything. I said I would tell you sometime about a sacrifice I was forced to make. I'll tell you now if you will not speak of what I say."

How delicious to have her confidence in anything. Vic smiled assent.

"My father had a fortune from my mother. When he died he left me to the care of my two uncles, and gave all his money to endow chairs in universities. He thought a woman could marry money, and that he was doing mankind a service in this endowment. Maybe he was, but I've always rebelled against being dependent. I've always wanted my own. Uncle Joshua thinks I am frivolous, and he has told Uncle Lloyd that it's just my love of spending and extravagant notions that makes me rebel against conditions. It is n't. It's the sense of being robbed, as it were. It was n't right and honest toward me, even in a great cause, to leave me dependent. Uncle Lloyd would never have done it. I hope he does n't think I'm as bad as Uncle Joshua does. You won't mind my telling you this, nor think me ungrateful to my relatives for their care of me. Nobody quite understands me but you."

The time had come for them to join the jolly picnic crowd in the Corral. She would go back to Vincent Burgess in a little while, and this glorious day would be only a memory. And yet, down in the pretty glen, Victor had held her hands and kissed her red lips. And she had been glad down there. The void in his life seemed blacker than the blackness behind the cavern.

"Elinor," he asked, suddenly, "are you bound by any promise—has Professor Burgess—?" He hesitated.

"No," she answered, turning her face away.

"Pardon my rudeness. You know I am not well-bred," he said, gently.

"Victor Burleigh, you ill-bred, of all the gentle, manly fellows in Sunrise! You know you are not."

A great hope leaped to life now, as Vic recalled the query, "If Victor Burleigh had his corners knocked off and was sandpapered down and had money?"—and of Elinor's blushing confession that it would make a difference she could not help if these things were. The corners were knocked off now, and Dean Fenneben had gently but persistently applied the sandpaper. The money must be henceforth the one condition.

"Elinor." Vic's voice was sweet as low bars of music.

"Oh, Victor, there's something I can't prevent."

She was thinking of Uncle Joshua, whose money had supported her all these years and of her obligation to heed his wishes. It was all settled for her now. And all the while Victor was thinking of his own limited means as the rock that was wrecking him with her.

For all his life afterward he never forgot the sorrow of that moment. He looked into Elinor's face, and all the longing, all the heart-hunger of the days gone by, and of the days to come seemed to lie in those wide-open eyes shaded by long black lashes.

"Elinor, my father's cruel murder and my mother dying alone were one kind of grief. My fight with those deadly poison things to rescue little Bug was another kind. My days of hardship and poverty on the claim, with only Bug and me in that desolate loneliness, was still another. But none of these seem a sorrow beside what I must face henceforth. And yet I have one joy mine now. You did care down in the glen. May I keep that one gracious joy—mine always?"

"You have always won in every game. You will in this struggle. Don't forget the name your mother gave you." Her eyes were luminous with tears. "We must go down to the Corral now. Tomorrow will make things all right. I shall be proud of you and your success everywhere, for you will succeed."

"I may not be worthy of victory," he said, sadly.

"You have never been unworthy. Don't be now." She smiled bravely.

They turned from the west prairie and the sunset, and slowly they passed out of its passing radiance down to the darkening spaces of the old Kickapoo Corral.

And the day with its gladness and sorrow, whether for loss or gain, slipped into the shadowy beauty of an April twilight.

## CHAPTER IX. GAIN, OR LOSS?

Ye know how hard an Idol dies, an' what that meant   to
me—E'en take it for a sacrifice, acceptable to Thee.
             —KIPLING

THE ball game on Friday, the thirteenth, was a great event this year. The Sunrise football eleven had held the championship record with an uncrossed goal line in the autumn. The basket-ball team had had no defeat this year. Debating tests had given Sunrise the victory. That came through Trench and the crippled student. And the state oratorical struggle repeated the story, a conquest, all the greater because Victor Burleigh, the athlete, wore also the laurels of oratory. And why should he not, with that fine presence and magnificent voice? As Dr. Fenneben listened to his forceful logic he saw clearly the line for the boy's future, a line, he thought, that could end at last only in the pulpit.

One more battle to fight now and Lagonda Ledge and the whole Walnut Valley would go down in history as famous soil. It was a banner year for Sunrise, and enthusiasm was at fever pitch, which in college is the only healthy temperature. In this last battle Sunrise turned again to Victor Burleigh as its highest hope. Although this was his first game for the season, he had never failed to bring victory to the Sunrise banners, and in all his base-ball practice he was as unerring as he was speedy. And then success was his habit anyhow. So "Burleigh at the bat" was the slogan now from the summit of the college ridge to the farthest corners of Lagonda Ledge; and idol worship were insignificant compared to the adulation poured out on him. And Burleigh, being young and very human, had all the pleasure the adoration of a community can bring to its local hero. For truly, few triumphs in life's later years can be fraught with half the keen joy these school day victories bring. And the applause of listening senates means less than good old comrades' yells.

Vincent Burgess, A.B., Greek Professor from Boston, seemed to have forgotten entirely about types and geographical breadths and seclusion for profound research amid barren prairies. He was faculty member on the Athletic board now and enthusiastic about all college sports. Sunrise had done this much for him anyhow. In addition, the young educator was taking on a little roundness, suggestive of a stout form in middle life.

But Vincent Burgess had not forgotten all of the motives that had pulled him Kansas-ward, although unknown to Dr. Fenneben, he had already refused to consider a position higher up in an eastern college. He was not quite ready to leave the West yet. Of course, not. Elinor Wream was only half through school and growing more popular as she was growing more womanly and more beautiful each year. His salvation lay in keeping on the grounds if he would hold his claim undisturbed.

Burgess had come to Kansas, he had told Fenneben, in order to know something of the state where his only sister had lived. He did not know yet all he wished to know about her life and death here. Her name was never spoken in his father's presence after she came West, so great was that father's anger over her leaving the East. And deep in Vincent's mind he fixed the impression that his daughter had died as unreconciled to her brother as to her father himself.

This was all his own business, however, and hidden deep, almost out of sight of himself, was a selfish motive that had not yet put a visible mark on the surface.

Burgess wanted to marry Norrie Wream, and he wanted her to have all the good things of life which in her simple rearing had been denied her. The heritage from his father's estate included certain trust funds ambiguously bestowed by an eccentric English ancestor upon someone who had come West not long before his death. These funds Vincent held by his father's will—to which will Joshua Wream was witness—on condition that no heir to these funds was living. If there were such person or persons living—but Burgess knew there were none. Joshua Wream had made sure of that for him before he left Cambridge. And yet it might be well to stay in Kansas for a year or two—much better to settle any possible difficulty here than to have anything follow him East later. For Burgess had his eye on Dr. Wream's chair in Harvard when the old man should give it up. That was a part of the contract between the two men, the old doctor and the young professor. Until the night when Bond Saxon forced him to take an unwilling oath, Burgess had had a comfortable conscience, sure that his financial future was settled, and confident that this assured him the hand of Elinor Wream when the time was ripe. With that October night, however, a weight of anxiety began that increased with the passing days. For as he grew nearer to the student life and took on flesh and good will and a broader knowledge of the worth of humanity, so he grew nearer to this smoothly hidden inner care. And, outside and in, he wanted to stay in Kansas for the time.

In the weeks before the big ball game, Victor Burleigh seemed to have forgotten the glen and the west bluff above the Kickapoo Corral. The girls who would have substituted for Elinor in the afternoon ramble took up much of the big sophomore's time, and he never seemed more gay nor care free. And Elinor, if she had a heartache, did not show it in her happy manner.

On the afternoon before the ball game, a May thunderstorm swept the Walnut Valley and the darkness fell early. As Dennie Saxon waited on the Sunrise portico before starting out in the rain, Professor Burgess locked the front door and joined her. Victor Burleigh was also waiting beside a stone column for the shower to lighten. Burgess did not see him in the darkening twilight and Burleigh never spoke to the young instructor when it was not necessary.

"I must be nervous," Professor Burgess said, trying to manage Dennie's umbrella and catching it in her hair. "I had a letter today that worried me."

"Too bad!" Dennie said sympathetically.

"I'll tell you all about it sometime."

He was trying to loose the wire rib-joint from Dennie's hair, which the dampness was rolling in soft little ringlets about her forehead and neck. Half-consciously, he remembered the same outline of rippling hair, as it had looked in the glow of the October camp fire down in the Kickapoo Corral when she was telling the old legend of Swift Elk and The Fawn of the Morning Light. She smiled up at him consolingly. Dennie was level-headed, and life was always worth living where she was.

"I'll be your rain beau." He took her arm to assist her down the steps.

So courteous was his action, she might have been a lady of rank instead of old Bond Saxon's daughter carrying her own weight of a sorrow greater than Lagonda Ledge dreamed of. As the two walked slowly homeward under the dripping shelter of the trees, Vincent Burgess felt a sense of comfort and pleasure out of all keeping for a man in love elsewhere. Victor Burleigh watched them from the shadow of the portico column.

"I believe Trench is right. He insists that Burgess likes Dennie, or that he is mean enough to deceive Dennie into liking him. A man like that ought to be killed—a scholar, and a rich man, and Dennie such a brave little poor girl with a kind, weak-kneed, old father on her heart. Norrie ought to know this, but who am I to say a word?"

"Victor Burleigh, won't you release the fair princess from the tower?" a girl's voice called.

Vic turned to see Elinor framed in the half-way window of the south turret. And in that dripping shadowy light, no frame could want a rarer picture.

"I've fallen into the pit and am far on the road to perdition," Elinor said. "I hurried down this way from choir practice and Uncle Lloyd's gone and left the lower door locked. It thundered so, and Dennie didn't come into the study, and nobody heard my screams. But if I perish, I perish," she added with mock resignation.

"If you'll let up on perishing for half a minute, Rapunzel, I'll to the rescue," Vic cried, "if I have to climb the dome and knock the *per aspera* out of the State Seal and come down through the hole, *per astra ad aspera*." And then he rushed off to find an unlocked exit to the building.

From the Chapel end of the circular stairs, he called presently.

"Curfew must not ring for a couple of seconds. Rise to the surface, fair mermaid."

Elinor came up the winding stair into the dimly lighted chapel at his call. The two had avoided each other since the April day in the glen. They were not to blame for this chance meeting now.

"When you are in trouble and the nights are dark and rainy, call me, Elinor," Vic said as they were crossing the rotunda.

"If I show you sometimes how to look up and find the light, as you showed me the Sunrise beacon on the night of the storm out on West Bluff, you may be glad you heard me. See that glow on the dome! You would have missed that down in Lagonda Ledge."

A level ray from a momentary cloudrift in the western sky smote the stained glass of the dome, lighting its gleaming inscription with a fleeting radiance.

"But the light comes rarely and is so far away, and between times, only the cave, and the dark ways behind it leading to the river," he said gravely. The sorrow of hopelessness was his tone.

"Not unless one chooses to burrow downward," she replied softly. "Let's hurry home. Tomorrow you will be 'Victor the Famous' again. I hope this shower won't spoil the ball game."

As night deepened, the rain fell steadily. Up in Victor Burleigh's room Bug Buler grew drowsy early.

"I want to say my pwayers now, Vic," he said.

The big fellow put down his book and took the child in his arms. Bug had a genius for praying briefly and for others rather than for himself. Tonight he merely clasped his chubby hands and said, reverently:

"Dear Dod, please ist make Vic dood as folks finks he is, for Thwist's sake. Amen-n-n."

When he fell asleep, Victor sat a long while staring at the window where the May rain was beating heavily. At length, he bent over little Bug and pushed back the curls from his brow. Bug smiled up drowsily and went on sleeping.

"As good as folks think I am, Bug!" he mused. "You have gotten between me and the rattlesnakes that were after my soul a good many times, little brother-of-mine. As good as folks think I am! Do you know what it costs to be that good?"

Ten minutes later he sat in Lloyd Fenneben's library.

"I have come for help," he said in reply to the Dean's questioning face.

"I hope I can give it," Fenneben responded.

"It's about tomorrow's game. There are sure to be some professional players on the other team. I want Sunrise to win. I want to win myself." Vic's voice was harsh tonight. And the Dean caught the hard tone.

"I want Sunrise to win. I want you to win. There will probably be some professionals to play against, but we have no way of proving this," Fenneben said.

"What do you think of such playing, Doctor?" Vic asked.

"I think the rule about professionalism is often a strained piece of foolishness. It is violated persistently and persistently winked at, but so long as it is the rule there is only one square thing to do, and that is to live up to the law. You should not dread any professionalism in the game tomorrow, however. You'll bring us through anyhow, and keep the Sunrise name and fame untarnished." The Dean smiled genially.

Burleigh's face was very pale and a strange fire burned in his eyes.

"Dr. Fenneben"—his musical voice rang clear—"I'm only a poor devil from the short-grass country where life each year depends on that year's crop. Three years out of four, the wind and drouth bring only failure at harvest time. Then we starve our bodies and grip onto hope and determination with our souls till seedtime comes again. I want a college education. Last summer burned us out as usual within a month of harvest. Then the mortgage got in its work on my claim and I had to give it up. I had barely enough to get through here at pauper rates this year—but I could n't do it and keep Bug, too. I went into Colorado and played baseball for pay, so I could come here and bring him with me. That's why I can out-bat our team, and could win dead easy for Sunrise tomorrow. Nobody in Kansas knows it. Now, what shall I do?"

The words were shot out like bullets.

"What shall you do?" Lloyd Fenneben's black eyes held Burleigh. "There is only one thing to do. When you ranked high in grades with only the trivial matter of excusable absence against you—no broken law—you took Professor Burgess gently by the throat and told him you meant to play anyhow. You stood your ground like a man, for your own sake and for the honor of Sunrise. Stand like a man for your own sake and the honor of Sunrise, now. Go to Professor Burgess and take him gently—by the hand, this time—and tell him you do not mean to play, and why you cannot."

Burleigh sat still as stone, his face white as marble, his wide-open eyes under his black brows seeing nothing.

"But our proud record—the glorious honor of this college," he said at length, and back of his words was the thought of Victor Burleigh, the idol of Sunrise, dethroned, where he had been adored.

"There is no honor for a college like the honesty of its students. There is no prouder record than the record of daring to do the right. You could get into the game once by a brute's strength. Get out of it now by a gentleman's honor."

Behind the speech was Lloyd Fenneben himself, sympathetic, firm, upright, before whom the harshness of Victor Burleigh's face slowly gave place to an expression of sorrow.

"My boy," Fenneben said gently, "Nature gave us the Walnut Valley with its limestone ledges and fine forest trees. But before our Sunrise could be builded the ledge had to be shapen into the hewn stone, the green tree to the seasoned lumber, quarter-sawed oak—quarter-sawed, mind you. Mill, forge and try-pit, ax and saw and chisel, with cleft and blow and furnace heat, shaped them all for Service. Over our doorway is the Sunrise initial. It stands also for Strife, part of which you know already; but it stands for Sacrifice as well. You are in the shaping. God grant you may be turned out a man fitted by Sacrifice for Service when the shaping is done."

Burleigh rose, silent still, and the two went out together. At the doorway, he turned to Fenneben, who grasped his hand without a word. And once again, the firm hand clasp of the Dean of Sunrise seemed to bind the country boy to the finer things of life. It had done the same on that day after the Thanksgiving game when he sat in Fenneben's study, and understood for the first time what gives the right to pride in brawny arm and steel-spring nerve.

After Burleigh left him, Lloyd Fenneben stood for a long time on his veranda in the light of the doorway watching the steady downpour of the warm May rain. As he turned at length to enter the house a rough-looking man with rain-soaked clothing and slouched hat, sprang out of the shadows.

"Stranger," he called hastily. "There's a little child fell in the river round the bend, and his mother got hold of him, but she can't pull him out, and can't hold on much longer. Will you come help me, quick? I've only got one arm or I would n't have had to ask for help."

An empty sleeve was flapping in the rain, and Fenneben did not notice then that the man kept that side of himself all the time in the shadows. Fenneben had only one thought as he hurried away in the darkness, to save the woman and child. His companion said little, directing the course toward the bend in the river before the gateway of Pigeon Place. As they pushed on with all speed through rain and mud, Fenneben was hardly conscious that Dennie Saxon's words about the lonely gray-haired hermit woman were recurring curiously to his mind.

"If talking about Sunrise made her cry like that, maybe you might do something for her," Dennie had said. He had never tried to do anything for her. Somehow she seemed to be the woman who was in peril now, and he was half-consciously blaming himself that he had never tried to help her, had not even thought of her for months.

Women were not in his line, except the kindly impersonal interest he felt for all the Sunrise girls, and his sense of responsibility for Norrie, and the memory of a girl—oh, the hungry haunting memory!

All this in a semi-conscious fleetness swept across his mind, that was bent on reaching the river, and on that woman holding a drowning child. At the bend in the river, the man halted suddenly.

"Look out! There's a stone; don't stumble!" he said hoarsely, dodging back as he spoke.

Then Fenneben was conscious of his own feet striking the slab of stone by the roadside, of a sudden shove from somebody behind him, a two-armed man it must have been, of stumbling blindly, trying to catch at the elm tree that stood there, of falling through the underbrush, headforemost, into the river, even of striking the water. As he fell, he was very faintly conscious of a sense of pity for Victor Burleigh fighting out a battle with his own honor tonight, and then he must have heard a dog's fierce yelp, and a woman's scream. Somehow, it seemed to come through distance of time, as out of past years, and not through length of space—and then of a brutal laugh and an oath with the words:

"Now for Josh Wream, and—"

But Fenneben's head had struck the stone ledge against which the Walnut ripples at low tide, and for a long time he knew no more.

It was raining still when Victor Burleigh reached the Saxon House. At the door he met Professor Burgess, who was just leaving. Strangely enough, the memory of their first meeting at the campus gate on a September day flashed into the mind of each as they came face to face now. They never spoke to each other except when it was necessary. And yet tonight, something made them greet each other courteously.

"Professor, will you be kind enough to come up to my room a few minutes?" Burleigh asked, lifting his cap to his instructor with the words.

"Certainly," Vincent Burgess said with equal grace.

Bug Buler had kicked off the bed covering and lay fast asleep on his little cot with his stubby arms bare, and his little fat hands, dimpled in each knuckle, thrown wide apart.

"I saw a picture like this once for the sign of the cross," Vic said as he drew the covering over the little form. "Bug has been a cross to me sometimes, but he's oftener my salvation."

Professor Burgess wondered again, why a boy like Burleigh should have been given a voice of such rare charm.

"I will not keep you long," Vic said, turning from Bug. "I cannot play in tomorrow's game, and be a man."

Then, briefly, he explained the reason.

"It is raining still. Take my umbrella," he said at the close of his simply told story. "But tomorrow's sunshine will dry the field for the game, all right. Good night."

"Good night," Vincent Burgess said hoarsely, and plunged into the darkness and the rain.

Ten steps from the Saxon House, he came plump into Bond Saxon, who staggered a little to avoid him.

"My luck on rainy nights," Vincent thought. "The old fellow's sprees seem to run with the storms. He hasn't been 'off' for a long time."

But Bond Saxon was never more sober in his life, and he clutched the young man's arm eagerly.

"Professor Burgess, won't you help me!" he cried.

"What do you want to do on a night like this?" Burgess asked, remembering the vow he had been forced to make, by this same man.

"Come help me save a man's life!" Bond urged.

"Look here, Saxon. You've got some wild notion out of a boot-legger's bottle. Straighten up now. It's an infamous thing in a college town like Lagonda Ledge, where neither a saloon nor a joint would be allowed, that some imp of Satan should forever be bringing you whisky. Who does it, anyhow?"

"I'm not drunk and haven't been for six months. Come on, for God's sake, and help me to save a life, maybe two lives, from the very man that's done the boot-leggin' and robbin' in this town for months and months." Saxon's words were convincing enough.

"What can I do?" Burgess asked. "I'm not a policeman."

"Come on! Come on!" Saxon urged, tugging at the professor's arm. "It 's a life, I tell you."

Vincent yielded unwillingly, the night, the beating rain, the man who asked it of him, the purpose, his own unfitness—all holding him back. Before they had gone far, Bond Saxon suddenly exclaimed:

"Say, Professor, do you remember the night I asked you to take care of Dennie if anything should happen to me?"

"Do YOU remember it?" Burgess responded. "You didn't ask; you demanded."

"I was drunk then. I'm sober now. Burgess, if anything should happen to me now, would you still be willing?" Bond Saxon asked in tense anxiety.

"I've already taken oath," Burgess said. "I think your daughter may need somebody's care before anything happens if you keep up this gait."

They hurried on through the rain until they had left the board walk and the town lights, and were staggering along the cinder-made path, when Burgess halted.

"Saxon, who's the man, or two men, you want to save? I believe you are drunk."

Bond Saxon grasped his arm, and said hoarsely:

"Don't shriek here. We are in danger, now. It's not two men. It's a man and a woman, maybe. It's Dean Funnybone. Come on!"

## CHAPTER X. THE THIEF IN THE MOUTH

O, thou invisible spirit of wine, if thou hast no, name to be
known by, let us call thee, devil!
—SHAKESPEARE

WHEN Lloyd Fenneben could think again, the waters had receded,
the rock ledge had turned to a pillow under his head, the river bank
was a straight white hospital wall, sunlight and sweet air for the
darkness and the rain, and Norrie Wream was beside him instead of
the brutal stranger. His heavy black hair was shorn away and his
head was bound with much soft cotton stuffs. His left arm was full
of prickles, as if the blood had just resumed circulation.

"And meantime?" he said, looking up at Elinor.

"Yes, meantime, it's June time," Elinor replied.

"Well, and what of Sunrise? Did we—"

"Oh, yes, we did. The college first. The ruling passion, strong in the
hospital. When a Wream gets to kingdom-come, he always asks
Saint Peter first for a mortar board and gown instead of a crown and
wings." Norrie's eyes were shining. "And he's a little particular
about the lining of the wings, too—Purple, for Law; White, for
Letters; Blue, for Philosophy; Red, for Divinity. Take this quieting
powder. College presidents should be seen and not heard." She
smilingly silenced him.

Under her gentle ministrations, Dr. Fenneben could picture what
comfort might be in store for Vincent Burgess in a day, doubtless
only two years away. He resented Joshua Wream's estimate of
Elinor. Surely Joshua had never seen her in the place of nurse.

"Now, meantime, Uncle Lloyd," Elinor was saying, "commencement
passed off beautifully under Acting-Dean Burgess, considering how
sad and heavy-hearted everybody was. The trustees want to raise
Professor Burgess's salary next year—he's so competent."

Lloyd Fenneben's eyes were not bandaged, and as he looked at Elinor he wondered at her utter lack of reserve and sentiment, when she spoke of Burgess in such a frank, matter-of-fact way. When he was in love years ago—but times must have changed.

"The arrangements for next year are all looked after. Everything will be done exactly as you would have it done. There's not one thing to put a worry into that cotton round your head."

"Good! Now, tell me of 'beforehand.'" His smile was as charming as ever.

"In your fever you've been telling us about a one-armed man who had two arms to push people into the river, of his wanting you to save some child's life, and of your stumbling over the stone. That's all we know about that. Bond Saxon and Professor Burgess found you in the water at the north bend in the Walnut close to that hermit woman's house. Either you fell in, or somebody pushed you down the bank, headforemost, and you struck a ledge of rock." Elinor's eyes were full of tears now. "You would have been drowned, if that white-haired woman had n't jumped in and held your head above water while she clung to the bushes with one hand. Her dog helped, too, like a real hero. It stood on the bank and held to her shawl that she had fastened round you to hold you. And the river was rising so fast, too. It was awful. I don't know just how it was all managed, Uncle Lloyd, but it was managed between the woman and her dog at first, and Professor Burgess and Bond Saxon at last, and you are safe now, and on the high road, the very elevated tracks, to recovery. When your fever was the highest, the doctors kept telling me about your splendid constitution and your temperate life. You must get well now."

She bent over him and softly caressed his hand.

"Where is that woman now? Dennie Saxon asked me once to do something for her in her loneliness. She got ahead of my negligence and did something for me, it seems."

"She left Lagonda Ledge the very day they rushed us up here to the hospital. Is n't she strange? And she is so gentle and sweet, but so sad. I never saw such apathetic face as hers, Uncle Lloyd."

"When did you see her?" Fenneben asked.

"She came to ask after you. Nobody thought you would get over it." Elinor's voice trembled. "The fever was burning you up and it took three doctors to hold you. I saw her face when Dennie Saxon said they thought you wouldn't pull through. Your own sister couldn't have turned whiter, Uncle Lloyd."

"And the one-armed man I seemed to remember?"

"I don't know. I've been too busy to ask many questions. Lagonda Ledge is in mourning for you. It will run up the flag above half-mast when I write how much better you are. Bond Saxon has a theory that some thief wanted to rob you and decoyed you away on pretense of helping somebody out of the river. You are an easy mark, Uncle."

"Why should Bond Saxon have a theory? And how did he know where to find me? And how did that gray-haired woman and her dog happen in on the scene just then? This is a grim sort of dime novel business, Norrie. Things don't fall out this way in real life unless there is some reason back of them. I think I'll bear investigating."

"I think so myself—you or your romantic rescuing squad. You might call the dog to the witness stand first, for he was the first on the scene. I forgot though that the dog is dead. They found him down the river with his throat cut. The plot thickens." Elinor's frivolous spirit was returning with the lessening of care.

"Tell me about the ball game," Fenneben said next.

"Oh, it rained for hours and hours, and there wasn't any train service for Lagonda Ledge for a week, and all the Inter-Collegiate Athletic events for the season were called off for Sun rise-by-the-Walnut."

"And the students, generally?" Dr. Fenneben questioned.

"Mr. Trench will be back," Elinor exclaimed, "and folks have just found out that it's old Trench who's keeping that crippled boy in school, the one they call 'Limpy.' Trench rustles jobs for him and divides his own income for college expenses with the boy for the rest of the cost. I don't know how the story got out, but I asked him about it when he was up here to see you. He just grinned and drawled lazily, 'I can save a little on shoe leather, that some fellows wear out hurrying so, and I don't burst up so many hats with a swelled head as some do. So I keep a little extra change on these accounts. We're going down to Oklahoma when we graduate. Limpy's going to be a Methodist preacher and I a stockman. I'll keep him in raw material for converts out of the cowboys I'll have to handle.' Isn't old Trenchy a hero? He says Dean Funnybone showed him how to think about somebody else beside Trench a little bit."

"Oh, yes; Trench is a hero and I've known about that whole thing for a long while," the Dean asserted. "And Victor Burleigh?"

A shadow in the beautiful dark eyes, a half-tone lowering of the voice, and a general indifference of manner, as Elinor answered:

"I'm sure I don't know anything about him, except that he's coming back next year."

Dr. Fenneben read the whole story in the words and manner of the answer, and he smiled grimly as he thought of Burgess and of the conflict of Wream against Wream if Elinor and his brother Joshua ever came to the clash of arms. But he was too weak now to direct matters.

And meantime, while Lagonda Ledge was holding its breath in anxiety and dread, and all the churches were joining in union prayer service for the life of their beloved Dean Fenneben, and the college year was ending in a halting between hope and dread—meantime, the same queries of Dr. Fenneben as to motives were also queries in Professor Burgess' mind.

To the school and the town Dr. Fenneben's recovery was the only thing asked for. There was as yet no clew regarding the cause of the assault. Bond Saxon had avoided Burgess since the event, so the

# A Master's Degree

young man himself made occasion to get Bond up into Dr. Fenneben's study one June day just before commencement.

"Saxon," he said gravely, "you are a man of sense, and you know that there's something wrong about this Fenneben assault. You've put up some smooth stories about our happening to be out at the bend of the river that night, so I guess suspicion will be turned from us all right when Lagonda Ledge gets time to think about causes; but I must be let into the truth now." Burgess was adamant now.

For a little while the old man looked away through the study window at the prairie empire to be found for the looking.

"Do you see that little twist of blue smoke over west?" he queried presently.

"What of it?" Burgess asked.

"Nothing, only the man huddlin' down round the fire makin' that smoke way down where it's cold and dark, that's the man who—say, Professor!"

Old Bond looked up appealingly, and the pitiful face touched Burgess' heart.

"What is it, Saxon? Be frank now, but be fair, too. Sooner or later, this thing must be run down. Fenneben will do it himself, anyhow, as soon as he's well enough."

"Professor, I have asked you twice if you'd be good to Dennie—"

"Yes, yes; you always come back to that. Anybody would be good to her, and she's a capable girl who does n't need anybody's care, anyhow. Now, go on."

"I will"—it seemed an heroic resolve—"I asked this for Dennie, because my own life is never safe."

"So you have said. Why not?" Burgess insisted. There was no way to evade the question now.

"That's my own business—just a little longer," Bond answered slowly. "One thing more; I want your promise not to tell what I say—yet awhile. It can't hurt anyone to keep still, and it will help some folks."

"Oh, I'll help you all I can." Burgess's kindly patience now was strangely unlike the aristocratic, resentful man to whom old Bond Saxon had appealed one stormy October night.

"I'm a failure, Professor. I've spoiled my life by my infernal weak will and appetite for whisky. I know it as well as you do. But I'm not meant for a bad man." There was unspeakable pathos in Saxon's face and words.

"Nobody would call you bad. You are a lovable man when you— keep straight," Burgess declared cordially.

"I graduated from the university back in the sixties," Bond went on.

"You!" Burgess exclaimed.

"Yes, I'm one of your alumni brothers from Harvard. It takes more 'n a college diploma to make a man sometimes, although this would mighty soon get to be a cheap, destructible nation, if we should pull the colleges out of it. The boys I've seen Sunrise make into men does an old man's heart good to think about! But there's more than book-learning in a Master's Degree. There must be MASTERY in it. I never got farther 'n an A.B., partly because Nature made me easy going, but mostly because whisky ruined me. I finally came to Kansas. I'd have had tremens long ago but for that. But even here a man's got to keep the law inside, or no human law can prevent his making a beast of himself."

Saxon paused, and the professor waited.

"The man that sets the cussed trap for me is a law breaker, an escaped convict, and a murderer. That's what drinking did for him; drinking and injustice in money matters together."

Burgess started and his face grew pale.

"Oh, it's a fact, Professor. There are several roads to ruin. One by the route I've taken. One may be too much love of money, of women, or of having your own way. You can ruin your soul by getting it set on one thing above everything else. Education, for instance, like the Wreams back there in Cambridge."

"The Wreams!" Burgess exclaimed.

"Yes, old Joshua Wream sold himself to an appetite for musty old Sanscrit till he'd sacrifice anybody's comfort and joy for it, same as I sold out to a fool's craving for drink. You'll know the Wreams sometime as I know 'em now. Fenneben's only a stepbrother and the West made a man of him. He was always a gentleman."

"Go on!" Vincent's voice was hardly audible.

"This outlaw, boot-legger, thief, and murderer was a respectable fellow once, the adopted son of a wealthy family back East, who began by spoiling him, lavished money on him, and let him have his own way in everything. He was a gay youngster on the side, given to drinking and fast company. He fell in love with a pretty girl, but when she found him out, she cut him. Then he went to the dogs, blaming her because she had sense enough to throw him over where he belonged. She fell in love—the right kind of love—with another man. And this young fool who had no claim on her at all, swore vengeance. Her family wanted her to marry the young sport because he had money. They were long on money—her father was, anyhow. But she would n't do it."

"Did she marry the one she really cared for?" Burgess asked eagerly.

"No; but that's another story. Meantime this fellow's father died, leaving the boy he, himself, had started on the wrong road, entirely out of his will. The boy went to the devil—and he's still there."

Saxon paused and looked once more at the tiny wavering smoke column, hardly visible now.

"He's over yonder hiding away from the light of day under the bluffs by the fire that sends that curl of smoke up through the crevices in the rock, an outlaw thief."

Saxon gazed long at the landscape beyond the Walnut. When he spoke again, it was with an effort.

"Professor, this outlaw got a hold on me once when I was drunk, drunk by his making. It would do no good to tell you about that. You could n't help me, nor harm him. You'll trust me in this?"

A picture of Dennie down in the Kickapoo Corral, with the flickering firelight on her rippling hair, the weird, shadowy woodland, and the old Indian legend all came back to the young man now, though why he could not say.

"I certainly would never bring harm to you nor yours," he said kindly.

"I can't inform on the scoundrel. I can only watch him. The woman he was in love with years ago, who would n't stand for his wild ways—that's the gray-haired woman at Pigeon Place. Her life's been one long tragedy, though she is not forty yet."

The anguish on the old man's face was pitiful as he spoke.

"She has a reason of her own for living here, and she is the soul of courage. On the night of the Fenneben accident, I was out her way — yes, running away from Bond Saxon. I knew if I stayed in town, I'd get drunk on a bottle left at my door. So I tore out in the rain and the dark to fight it out with the devil inside of me. And out at Pigeon Place I run onto this fiend. When I ordered him back to his hiding place, he vowed he'd get Fenneben and put him in the river. There's one or two human things about him still. One is his fear of little children, and one is his love for that woman. He really did adore her years ago. I tracked home after him, and you know the rest. He put up some story to the Dean to entice him out there."

He hesitated, then ceased to speak.

"Why the Dean?" Burgess asked.

"Because Lloyd Fenneben's the man she loved years ago, and her folks wouldn't let her marry," Bond Saxon said sadly.

Burgess felt as if the limestone ridge was giving way beneath him.

"Where is she now?"

"She's gone, nobody knows where. I hope to heaven she will never come back," the old man replied.

"And it was she who saved Dr. Fenneben's life? Does he know who she is?"

"No, no. She's never let him know, and if she does n't want him to know, whose business is it to tell him?" Saxon urged. "I have hung about and protected her when she never knew I was near. But when I'm drunk, I'm an idiot and my mind is bent against her. I'd die to save her, and yet I may kill her some day when I don't know it." Bond Saxon's head was drooping pitifully low.

"But why live in such slavery? Why not tell all you know about this man and let the law protect a helpless woman?" Burgess urged.

Old Bond Saxon looked up and uttered only one word—"Dennie!"

Vincent Burgess turned away a moment. Dennie! Yes, there was Dennie.

"This woman had a husband, you say?" he asked presently.

Bond Saxon stared straight at him and slowly nodded his head.

"What became of him? Do you know?" Vincent questioned.

Saxon leaned forward, and, clutching Vincent Burgess by the arm, whispered hoarsely, "He's dead. I killed him. But I was drunk when I did it. And this man knows it and holds me bound."

## SERVICE

If you were born to honor, show it now;
if put upon you, make the judgment good that thought you worthy of it.
      —SHAKESPEARE

## CHAPTER XI. THE SINS OF THE FATHERS

They enslave their children's children who make
compromise with sin.
                    —LOWELL

IT was mid-December before Lloyd Fenneben saw Lagonda Ledge
again. In the murderous attempt upon his life, he had been hurled,
head-downward, upon the hidden rock-ledge with such force that
even his strong nervous system could barely overcome the shock.
Hours of unconsciousness were followed by a raging brain fever,
and paralysis, insanity, and death strove together against him. His
final complete recovery was slow, and he was wise enough to let
nature have ample time for rebuilding what had been so cruelly
wrenched out of line. It was this very patience and willingness to
take life calmly, when most men would have been in a fever of
anxiety about neglected business, that brought Lloyd Fenneben back
to Lagonda Ledge in December, a perfectly well man; and aside from
the holiday given in honor of the event, aside from the display of
flags and the big "Welcome" done in electric lights awaiting him at
the railroad station, where all the portable population of Lagonda
Ledge and most of the Walnut Valley, headed by the Sunrise
contingent, en masse, seemed to be waiting also—aside from the
demonstration and general hilarity and thanksgiving and rejoicing,
there seemed no difference between the Dean of the days that
followed and the Dean of the years before. His black hair was as long
and heavy as ever. His black eyes had lost nothing of their keenness.
His smile was just the same old, genial outbreak of good will, as he
heard the wildly enthusiastic refrain:

Rah for Funnybone!
Rah for Funnybone!
Rah for Funnybone!
Rah! RAH!! RAH!!!

It was twilight when the train pulled up to the station. The
December evening was clear and crisp as southern Kansas
Decembers usually are. The lights of the town were twinkling in the

dusk. Out beyond the river a gorgeous purple and scarlet after-sunset glow was filling the west with that magnificence of coloring only the hand of Nature dares to paint.

Several passengers left the train, but the company had eyes only for the Pullman car where Fenneben was riding. Nobody, except Bond Saxon, and a cab driver on the edge of the crowd, noticed a gray-haired woman who alighted so quietly and slipped to the cab so quickly that she was almost out to Pigeon Place before Fenneben had been able to clear the platform.

Behind the Dean was his niece, who halted on the car steps while her uncle went into the outstretched arms of Lagonda Ledge. At sight of her, the hats went high in air, as she stood there smiling above the crowd. It was Maytime when she went away. They had remembered her in dainty Maytime gowns. They were not prepared for her in her handsome traveling costume of golden brown, her brown beaver hat, and pretty furs. A beautiful girl can be so charming in her winter feathers. She had expected that Burgess would be first to meet her, and she was ready, she thought, to greet him, becomingly. But as the porter helped her to the platform, the crowd closed in, shutting him away momentarily, and a hand caught hers, a big, strong hand whose clasp, so close and warm, seemed to hold her hand by right of eternal possession. And Victor Burleigh's brown eyes full of a joyous light were looking down at her. It was all such a sweet, shadowy time that nobody crowding about them could see clearly how Elinor, with shining face, nestled involuntarily close to his arm for just one instant, and her low murmured words, "I am glad you were first," were lost to all but the big fellow before her, and a bigger, vastly lazy fellow, Trench, just behind her. It was Trench's bulk that had blocked the way for the professor a moment before. Then she was swallowed in the jolly greetings of goodfellowship, and Vincent Burgess carried her away to the carriage where her uncle waited.

"The thing is settled now," the young folks thought. But Dennie Saxon and Trench, who walked home together, knew that many things were hopelessly unsettled. By the law of natural fitness, Dennie and Trench should have fallen in love with each other. They were so alike in goodness of heart. But such mating of like with like, is rare, and under its ruling the world would grow so monotonously good, on the one hand, and bad, on the other, that life would be uninteresting.

During Dr. Fenneben's absence, Professor Burgess was acting-dean. For a man who, two years before, had never heard of a Jayhawker, who hoped the barren prairies would furnish seclusion for profound research in his library, and whose interest in the student body lay in its material to furnish "types," Dean Burgess, on the outside, certainly measured up well toward the stature of the real Dean— broad-minded, beloved "Funnybone."

And as Vincent Burgess grew in breadth of view and human interest, his popularity increased and his opportunities multiplied. Sunrise forgot that it had ever regarded him as a walking Greek textbook in paper binding. Next to Dr. Lloyd Fenneben, his place at Sunrise would be the hardest to fill now; and withal, sometime in the near future, there was waiting for him the prettiest girl that ever climbed the steps from the lower campus to the Sunrise door. Burgess had never dreamed that life in Kansas could be so full of pleasure for him.

And all the while, on the inside, another Burgess was growing up who quarreled daily with this happy outer Burgess. This inner man it was who held the secret of Bond Saxon's awful crime; the man who knew the life story of the would-be assassin of Lloyd Fenneben, and who knew the tragedy that had turned a fair-faced girl to a gray-haired woman, yet young in years. He knew the tragedy, but the woman herself he had never seen, save in the darkness and rain of that awful night when she had held Lloyd Fenneben's head above the fast rising waters of the Walnut. He had never even heard her voice, for he had sustained the limp body of Dr. Fenneben while Saxon helped the woman from the river and as far as to her own gate. But these were secret things outside of his own conscience. Inside of his conscience the real battle was fought and won, and lost, only to be won and lost over and over. So long as Elinor Wream was away, he could stay execution on himself. The same train that brought her home to Lagonda Ledge, brought a letter to Professor Vincent Burgess, A.B. The letter heading bore as many of Dr. Joshua

Wream's titles as space would permit, but the cramped, old-fashioned handwriting belonged to a man of more than fourscore years, and it was signed just "J. R."

Burgess read this letter many times that night after he returned from dinner at the Fenneben home. And sometimes his fists were clinched and sometimes his blue eyes were full of tears. Then he remembered little Bug, who had declared once that "Don Fonnybone was dood for twoubleness."

"I can't take this to Fenneben," he mused, as he read Joshua Wream's letter for the tenth time. "Nor can I go to Saxon. He's never sure of himself and when he's drunk, he reverses himself and turns against his best friends. And who am I to turn to a man like Bond Saxon for my confidences?"

"What about Elinor?" came a voice from somewhere. "The woman you would make your wife should be the one to whose loving sympathy you could turn at any of life's angles, else that were no real marriage."

"Elinor, of all people in the world, the very last. She shall never know, never!" So he answered the inward questioner.

Dimly then rose up before him the picture of Victor Burleigh on the rainy May night when he stood beside little Bug Buler's bed — Victor Burleigh, with his white, sorrowful face, and burning brown eyes, telling in a voice like music the reason why he must renounce athletic honors in Sunrise.

Burgess had been unconsciously exultant over the boy's confession. It would put the confessor out of reach of any claim to Elinor's friendship when the truth was known about his poverty and his professional playing. And yet he had followed Bond Saxon's lead the more willingly that night that he was hating himself for rejoicing with himself.

On this December night, with Elinor once more in Lagonda Ledge, Victor Burleigh must come again to trouble him. What a price that boy must have paid for his honesty! But he paid it, aye, he paid it! And then the rains put out the game and nobody knew except

Burleigh and himself. Burgess almost resented the kindness of Fate to the heroic boy. But all this solved no problems for Vincent Burgess, except the realization that here was one fellow who had a soul of courage. Could he confide in Burleigh? Not in a thousand years!

In utter loneliness, Vincent Burgess put out his light and stared at the window. The street lamps glowed in lonely fashion, for it was very late, and nobody was abroad. Up on the limestone ridge, the Sunrise beacon shone bravely. Down in town beside the campus gate—he could just catch a glimpse of one steady beam. It was the faithful old lamp in the hallway of the Saxon House, and beyond that unwavering light was Dennie.

"Dennie! Why have I not thought of her? The only one in the world whom I can fully trust. That ought to be a man's sweetheart, I suppose, but she is not mine. She is just Dennie. Heaven bless her! I've sworn to care for her. She must help me now." And with the comforting thought, he fell asleep beside the window.

The December sunset was superb in a glory of endless purple mists and rose-tinted splendor of far-reaching skies. The evening drops down early at this season and the lights were gleaming here and there in the town where the shadows fall soonest before the day's work is finished up in Sunrise.

Victor Burleigh, who had been called to Dr. Fenneben's study, found only Elinor there, looking out at the radiant beauty of the sunset sky beyond the homey shadows studded with the twinkling lights of Lagonda Ledge at the foot of the slope. The young man hesitated a little before entering. All day the school had been busy settling affairs for Professor Burgess and "Norrie, the beloved." Gossip has swift feet and from surmise to fact is a short course. Twenty-four hours had quite completely "fixed things" for Elinor Wream and Vincent Burgess, so far as Sunrise and Lagonda Ledge were able to fix them. So Burleigh, whose strong face carried no hint of grief, held back a minute now, before entering the study.

"I beg your pardon, Elinor. Dr. Fenneben sent for me."

Somehow the deep musical voice and her name pronounced as nobody else ever could pronounce it, and the big manly form and brave face, all seemed to complete the spell of the sunset hour. Elinor did not speak, but with a smile made room for him beside her at the window, and the two looked long at the deepening grandeur of the heavens and the misty shadows of heliotrope and silver darkening softly to the twilight below them.

"And God saw that it was good. And the evening and the morning were the fourth day," Victor said at last.

"Your voice grows richer with the passing years, Victor," Elinor said softly. "I wanted to hear it again the first time I heard you speak out there one September day."

"It is well to grow rich in something," Victor said, half-earnestly, half-carelessly.

Before Elinor could say more, they caught sight of Professor Burgess and Dennie Saxon, leaving the front portico as they had done on the May evening before the assault on Dr. Fenneben. Burgess and Dennie usually left the building together this year.

"Is n't Dennie a darling? Elinor said calmly.

"I guess so," he replied. "I don't just know what makes a girl a darling to another girl. I only know"—he was on thin ice now—"and I don't even know that very well."

They turned to the landscape again. The whole building was growing quiet. Footsteps were fading away down the halls. Doors clicked faintly here and there. Somebody was singing softly in the basement laboratory, and the sunset sky was exquisitely lovely above the quiet gray December prairies.

"It is too beautiful to last," Elinor said, turning to the young man beside her. "The joy of it is too deep for us to hold."

She did not mean to stay a moment longer, for all the scene could be hers forever in memory—imperishable!—and Victor did not mean to detain her. But her face as she turned from the window, the

119

hallowed setting of time and opportunity, and a heart-love hungering through hopeless, slow-dragging months, all had their own way with him. He put out his arms to her and she nestled within them, lifting a face to his own transfigured with love's sweetness. And he bent and kissed her red lips, holding her close in his arms. And in the shadowy twilight, with the faintly roseate banners of the sunset's after-glow trailing through it, for just one minute, heaven and earth came very near together for these two. And then they remembered, and Elinor put her hand in Victor's, who held it in his without a word.

Out in the hall, Trench with soft lazy step had just come to the study door in time to see and turn away unseen, and slowly pass out of the big front door, whistling low the while:

> My sweetheart lives on the prairies wide
>> By the sandy Cimarron,
> In a day to come she will be my bride,
>> By the sandy Cimarron.

Out by the big stone pillars of the portico, he looked toward the south turret and saw Dr. Fenneben as Vic had seen Elinor on the evening of the May storm. He did not call, but with a twist of the fingers as of unlocking a door, he dodged back into the building and up to the chapel end of the turret stairs to release the Dean.

Dr. Fenneben had started down to the study by the same old "road to perdition" stairs and paused at the window as Dennie and Burgess were passing out, unconscious of three pairs of eyes on them. Then the Dean saw down through the half-open study door the two young people by the window, and he knew he was not needed there. What that look in his black eyes meant, as he turned to the half-way window of the turret, it would have been hard to read. And the picture of a fair-faced girl came back to his own hungry memory. He was trying to calculate the distance from the turret window to the ground when Trench wig-wagged a rescue signal.

"You are a brick, Trench," he said, as the upper stairway door swung open to release him.

"You've the whole chimney," Trench responded, as he swung himself away.

Dr. Fenneben met Elinor in the rotunda.

"Wait a minute, Norrie, and I'll walk home with you."

In the study he met Burleigh, whose stern face was tender with a pathetic sadness, but there was no embarrassment in his glance. And Fenneben, being a man himself, knew what power for sacrifice lay back of those beautiful eyes.

"I can't give him the message I meant to give now. The man said there was no hurry. A veritable tramp he looked to be. I hope there is no harm to the boy in it. Why should a girl like Norrie love the pocketbook, and the things of the pocketbook, when a heart like Victor Burleigh's calls to her? I know men. I never shall know women." So he thought. Aloud he said: "I was detained, Burleigh, and I'll have to see you again. I have some matters to consider with you soon."

And Burleigh wondered much what "some matters" might be.

When Professor Burgess left Dennie he said, lightly:

"Miss Dennie, I need a little help in my work. Would you let me call this evening and talk it over with you? I don't believe anybody else would get hold of it quite so well."

Dennie had supposed this first evening after Elinor's return would find her lover making use of it. Why should Dennie not feel a thrill of pleasure that her services out-weighed everything else? Poor Dennie! She was no flirt, but much association with Vincent Burgess had given her insight to know that Norrie Wream would never understand him.

When Burgess returned to the Saxon House later in the evening, he met Bond Saxon at the door.

"Say, Professor, the devil will be to pay again. That Mrs. Marian is back. Got here on the same train Funnybone came on. And," lowering his voice, "he will be over there again," pointing toward the west bluffs. "He'll hound Funnybone to his doom yet. And she—she'll stand between 'em to the last. I told you one of the two human traits left in that beast is his fool fondness for that woman who wouldn't let him set foot on her ground if she knew it. It's a grim tragedy being played out here with nobody knowing but you and me."

"Saxon, I'm in no mood for all this tonight," Burgess said, "but for your daughter's sake keep away from the man's bottle now."

"Yes, for Dennie's sake—" Bond looked imploringly at Burgess.

"Yes, yes, I'll do my duty as I promised. But why not do it yourself toward her? Why not be a man and a father?"

"Me! A criminal! Do you know what that kind of slavery is?" Saxon whispered.

"Almost," Burgess answered, but the old man did not catch his meaning.

Dennie was waiting in the parlor, a cosy little room but without the luxurious appointments of Norrie Wream's home. Yet tonight Dennie seemed beautiful to Burgess, and this quiet little room, a haven of safety.

"Dennie," he said, plunging into his purpose at once. "I come to you because I need a friend and you are tempered steel."

Tonight Dennie's gray eyes were dark and shining. The rippling waves of yellow brown hair gave a sort of Madonna outline to her face, and there was about her something indefinably pleasant.

"What can I do for you, Professor Burgess?" she asked.

"Listen to me, Dennie, and then advise me."

Was this the acting-dean of Sunrise, a second Fenneben, already declared? His face was full of pathos, yet even in his feverish grief it seemed a better face to Dennie than the cold scholarly countenance of two years ago.

"My troubles go back a long way. My father was given to greed. He sold himself and my sister's happiness and mine for money. You think your father is a slave, Dennie, because he has a craving for whisky. Less than half a dozen times a year the demon inside gets him down."

Dennie looked up with a sorrowful face.

"Yes, but think of what he might do. You don't know what dreadful things he has done —"

"Yes, I do. He told me himself the very worst. I'll never betray him, Dennie. His punishment is heavy enough."

Burgess laid his hand on her dimpled hand in token of sincerity.

"But that's only rarely, little girl. My father every day in the year gave himself to an appetite for money till he cared for nothing else. My sister, who died believing that I also had turned against her, was forced to marry a man she did not love because he had money. I never knew the man she did love. It was a romance of her girlhood. I was away from home the most of my boyhood years, and she never mentioned his name after the affair was broken off. All I know is that she was deceived and made to believe some cruel story against him. She and her husband came West, where they died. My father never forgave them for going West, nor permitted me to speak her name to him. I never knew why until yesterday. My sister's husband had a brother out here with whom he meant to divide some possessions he had inherited. That settled him with my father forever. There was no DIVISION of property in his creed."

Burgess paused. Dennie's interest and sympathy made her silent company a comfort.

"I was heir to my father's estate, and heir also to some funds he held in trust. I was a scholar with ambition for honors — a Master's Degree and a high professional place in a great university. I trusted my whole life plans to the man who knew my father best — Dr. Joshua Wream."

Dennie looked up, questioningly.

"Yes, to Elinor's uncle, as unlike Dr. Fenneben as night and day."

"Do not blame me, Dennie, if two men have helped to misshape my life. My father believed that money is absolute. Dr. Wream holds scholarly achievement as the greatest life work. It has been Dr. Fenneben's part to show me the danger and the power in each."

It was dimly dawning on Burgess that the presence of Dennie, good, sensible Dennie, was a blessing outside of these things that could go far toward making life successful. But he did not grasp it clearly yet.

"Dr. Wream and I made a compact before I came West. It seemed fair to me then. By its terms I was assured, first, of my right to certain funds my father held in trust. It was Wream who secured these rights for me. Second, I was to succeed to his chair in Harvard if I proved worthy in Sunrise. In return I promised to marry Elinor Wream and to provide for her comfort and luxury with these trust funds my father and Wream had somehow been manipulating."

Oh, yes! Dennie was level-headed. And because she did not look up nor cry out Vincent Burgess did not see nor guess anything. His life had been a sheltered one. How could he measure Dennie's life-discipline in self-control and loving bravery?

"Elinor was heavy on Wream's conscience," Vincent went on, "because he and her father, Dr. Nathan Wream, took the fortune to endow colleges and university chairs that should have been hers from her mother's estate. You see, Dennie, there was no wrong in the plan. Elinor would be provided for by me. I would get up in my chosen profession. Nobody was robbed or defrauded. Joshua Wream's last years would be peaceful with his conscience at rest regarding Elinor's property. And, Dennie, who would n't want to marry Elinor Wream?"

"Yes, who wouldn't?" Dennie looked up with a smile. And if there were tears in her eyes Burgess knew they were born of Dennie's sweet spirit of sympathy.

"What is wrong, then?" she asked. "Is Elinor unwilling?"

"Elinor and I are bound by promises to each other, although no word has ever been spoken between us. It is impossible to make any change now. We are very happy, of course."

"Of course," Dennie echoed.

"I had a letter from Dr. Wream last night. A pitiful letter, for he's getting near the brink. Dennie—these funds I hold—I have never quite understood, but I had felt sure there was no other claimant. There was a clause in the strangely-worded bequest: 'for V. B. and his heirs. Failing in that, to the nearest related V. B.' It was a thing for lawyers, not Greek professors, to settle, and I came to be the nearest related V. B., Vincent Burgess, for I find the money belonged to my sister's husband, and I thought he left no heirs and I am the nearest related V. B. by marriage, you see?"

"Well?" Dennie's mind was jumping to the end.

"My sister married a Victor Burleigh, who came to Kansas to find his brother. Both men are dead now. The only one of the two families living is this brother's son, young Victor Burleigh, junior in Sunrise College. He knows nothing of his Uncle Victor, my brother-in-law— nor of money that he might claim. He belongs to the soil out here. Nobody has any claims on him, nor has he any ambition for a chair in Harvard, nor any promise to marry and provide for a beautiful girl who looks upon him as her future guardian."

Vincent Burgess suddenly ceased speaking and looked at Dennie.

"I cannot break an old man's heart. He implores me not to reveal all this, but I had to tell somebody, and you are the best friend a man could ever have, Dennie Saxon, so I come to you," he added presently.

"When did this Dr. Wream find out about Vic?" Dennie asked.

"A month ago. Some strange-looking tramp of a fellow brought him proofs that are incontestable," Burgess replied.

"And it is for an old man's peace you would keep this secret?" Dennie questioned.

"For him and for Elinor—and for myself. Don't hate me, Dennie. Elinor looks upon me as her future husband. I have promised to provide for her with the comforts denied her by her father, and I have lived in the ambition of holding that Harvard chair—Oh, it is all a hopeless tangle. I could never go to Victor Burleigh now. He would not believe that I had been ignorant of his claim all this time. He was never wrapped up in the pursuit of a career—Oh, Dennie, Dennie, what shall I do?"

He rose to his feet and Dennie stood up before him. He gently rested his hands on her shoulders and looked down at her.

"What shall you do?" Dennie repeated, slowly. "Whisky, Money, Ambition—the appetite that destroys! Vincent Burgess, if you want to win a Master's Degree, win to the Mastery of Manhood first. The sins of the fathers, yours and mine, we cannot undo. But you can be a man."

She had put her dimpled hands on his arms as they stood there, and the brave courage of her upturned face called back again the rainy May night, and the face of Victor Burleigh beside Bug Buler's cot, and his low voice as he said:

"I cannot play in tomorrow's game and be a man."

## CHAPTER XII. THE SILVER PITCHER

A picket frozen on duty—
  A mother starved for her brood—
  Socrates drinking the hemlock,
  And Jesus on the rood.
And millions who, humble and nameless,
  The straight hard pathway trod—
  Some call it Consecration,
  And others call it God.
    —WILLIAM HERBERT CARRUTH

"DR. FENNEBEN, I should like much to dismiss my classes for the afternoon," Professor Burgess said to the Dean in his study the next day.

"Very well, Professor, I am afraid you are overworked with all my duties added to yours here. But you don't look it," Fenneben said, smiling.

Burgess was growing almost stalwart in this gracious climate.

"I am very well, Doctor. What a beautiful view this is." He was looking intently now at the Empire that had failed to interest him once.

"Yes; it is my inspiration. 'Each man's chimney is his golden milestone,'" Fenneben quoted. "I've watched the smoke from many chimneys up and down the Walnut Valley during my years here, and later I've hunted out the people of each hearthstone and made friends with them. So when I look away from my work here I see friendly tokens of those I know out there." He waved his hand toward the whole valley. "And maybe, when they look up here and see the dome by day, or catch our beacon light by night, they think of 'Funnybone,' too. It is well to live close to the folks of your valley always."

"You are a wonderful man, Doctor," Burgess said.

"There are two 'milestones' I've never reached," the Doctor went on. "One is that place by the bend in the river. See the pigeons rising above it now. I wonder if that strange white-haired woman ever came back again. Elinor said she left Lagonda Ledge last summer."

"Where's the other place?" Burgess would change the subject.

"It i's a little shaft of blue smoke from a wood fire rising above those rocky places across the river. I've seen it so often, at irregular times, that I've grown interested in it, but I have missed it since I came back. It's like losing a friend. Every man has his vagaries. One of mine is this friendship with the symbols of human homes."

Burgess offered no comment in response. He could not see that the time had come to tell Fenneben what Bond Saxon had confided to him about the man below the smoke. So he left the hilltop and went down to the Saxon House. He wanted to see Dennie, but found her father instead.

"That woman's left Pigeon Place again," Saxon said. "Went early this morning. It's freedom for me when I don't have to think of them two. Thinking of myself is slavery enough."

Burgess loitered aimlessly about the doorway for a while. It was a mild afternoon, with no hint of winter, nor Christmas glitter of ice and snow about it. Just a glorious finishing of an idyllic Kansas autumn rounding out in the beauty of a sunshiny mid-December day. But to the man who stood there, waiting for nothing at all, the day was a mockery. Behind the fine scholarly face a storm was raging and there was only one friend whom he could trust — Dennie.

"Let's go walking, you and me!"

Bug Buler put up one hand to Burgess, while he clutched a little red ball in the other. Bug had an irresistible child voice and child touch, and Burgess yielded to their leading. He had not realized until now how lonely he was, and Bug was companionable by intuition and a stanch little stroller.

North of town the river lay glistening between its vine-draped banks. The two paused at the bend where Fenneben had been hurled almost to his doom, and Burgess remembered the darkness, and the rain, and the limp body he had held. He thought Fenneben was dead then, and even in that moment he had felt a sense of disloyalty to Dennie as he realized that he must think of Elinor entirely now. But why not? He had come to Kansas for this very thinking. It must be his life purpose now.

Today Burgess began to wonder why Elinor must have a life of ease provided for her and Dennie Saxon ask for nothing. Why should Joshua Wream's conscience be his burden, too? Then he hated himself a little more than ever, and duty and manly honor began their wrestle within him again.

"Let's we go see the pigeons," Bug suggested, tossing his ball in his hands.

Burgess remembered what Bond had said of the woman's leaving. There could be no harm in going inside, he thought. The leafless trees and shrubbery revealed the neat little home that the summer foliage concealed. Bug ran forward with childish curiosity and tiptoed up to a low window, dropping his little red ball in his eagerness.

"Oh, tum! tum!" he cried. "Such a pretty picture frame and vase on the table."

He was nearly five years old now, but in his excitement he still used baby language, as he pulled eagerly at Vincent Burgess' coat.

"It isn't nice to peep, Bug," Burgess insisted, but he shaded his eyes and glanced in to please the boy. He did not note the pretty gilt frame nor the vase beside it on the table. But the face looking out of that frame made him turn almost as cold and limp as Fenneben had been when he was dragged from the river. Catching the little one by the hand he hurried away.

At the gateway he lifted Bug in his arms.

He was not yet at ease with children.

"I dropped my ball," Bug said. "Let me det it."

"Oh, no; I'll get you another one. Don't go back," Burgess urged. "Do you know it is very rude to look into windows. Let's never tell anybody we did it; nor ever, ever do it again. Will you remember?"

"Umph humph! I mean, yes, sir! I won't fornever do it again, nor tell nobody." Bug buttoned up his lips for a sphinx-like secrecy. "Nobody but Dennie. And I may fordet it for her."

"Yes, forget it, and we'll go away up the river and see other things. Bug, what do you say when you want to keep from doing wrong?"

Bug looked up confidingly.

"I ist say, 'Dod, be merciless to me, a sinner'."

"Why not merciful, Bug?"

"Tause! If He's merciful it's too easy and I'm no dooder," Bug said, wisely.

"Who told you the difference?" Burgess asked.

"Vic. He knows a lot. I wish I had my ball, but let's go up the river."

"Out of the mouths of babes," Burgess murmured and hugged the little one close to him.

Victor Burleigh was in the little balcony of the dome late that afternoon fixing a defective wiring. Through the open windows he could see the skyline in every direction. The far-reaching gray prairie, overhung by its dome of amethyst bordered round with opal and rimmed with jasper, seemed in every blending tint and tone to call him back to Norrie. The west bluff above the old Kickapoo Corral in the autumn, the glen full of shadow-flecked light under the tender young April leaves, the December landscape as it lay beyond Dr. Fenneben's study windows — these belonged to Elinor. And all of them were blended in this vision of inexpressible grandeur, unfolded to him now from the dome's high vantage place.

"Twice Norrie has let me hold her in my arms and kiss her," he mused. "When I do that the third time it must be when there will be no remorse to hound me afterward." He looked down the winding

Walnut toward the whirlpool. "I'd rather swim that water than flounder here."

The sound of footsteps on the rotunda stairs made him turn to see Vincent Burgess just reaching the little balcony of the dome.

"I've come to have a word with you up here," he said. "We met once before in this rotunda."

"Yes, down there in the arena," Vic replied, recalling how like a beast he had felt then. "I was a young hyena that day. Bug Buler came just in time to save both of us. There is a comfort in feeling we can learn something. I've needed books and college professors to temper me to courtesy."

It was the only apology Vic had ever offered to Burgess, who accepted it as all that he deserved.

"We learn more from men than from books sometimes. I've learned from them how courageous a man may be when the need for sacrifice comes. Sit down, Burleigh, and let me tell you something."

They sat down on the low seat beside the dome windows. Overhead gleamed the message of high courage, *Ad Astra Per Aspera*. Below was the artistic beauty of the rotunda, where the evening shadows were deepening.

"We are higher than we were that other day. We care less for fighting as we get farther up, maybe," Burgess said, pleasantly.

"The only place to fight a man is in a cave, anyhow," Burleigh replied, looking at his brawny arms, nor dreaming how prophetic his words might be.

"We don't belong to that class of men now, whatever our far off ancestors may have been, but we are the sons of our fathers, Burleigh, and it is left to the living to right the wrongs the dead have begun."

Then, briefly, Vincent Burgess, A.B., Greek Professor from Harvard, told to Vic Burleigh from a prairie claim out beyond the Walnut, a part of what he had already told to Dennie Saxon, of the funds withheld from him so long. Told it in general terms, however, not shielding his father at all, but giving no hint that the first Victor Burleigh was his own brother-in-law. And of the compact with Joshua Wream and of Norrie he told nothing.

"Three days ago I did not know that you could be heir to this property," he concluded. "I've been interested in books and have left legal matters to those who controlled them for me."

He rose hastily, for Burleigh, saying nothing, was looking at him with wide-open brown eyes that seemed to look straight into his soul.

"I can restore your property to you. I cannot change the past. You have all the future in which to use it better than my father did, or I might have done. Goodnight."

He turned away and passed slowly down the rotunda stairs.

When he was gone Victor Burleigh turned to the open window of the dome. He was not to blame that the beautiful earth under a magnificent December sunset sky seemed all his own now.

"'If big, handsome Victor Burleigh had his corners knocked off and was sandpapered down,'" he mused. "Well, what corners I haven't knocked off myself have been knocked off for me and I've been sandpapered—Lord, I've been sandpapered down all right. I'm at home on a carpet now. 'And if he had money'." Vic's face was triumphant. "It has come at last—the money. And what of Elinor?"

The sacred memories of brief fleeting moments with her told him "what of Elinor."

"The barriers are down now. It is a glorious old world. I must hunt up Trench and then—"

He closed the dome window, looked a moment at the brave Kansas motto, radiant in the sunset light, and then, picking up his tools, he went downstairs.

"Hello, Trench I he called as he reached the rotunda floor. I must see you a minute."

"Hello, you Angel-face! Case of necessity. Well, look a minute," Trench drawled. "But that's the limit, and twice as long as I'd care to see you, although, I was hunting you. Funnybone wants to see you in there."

Victor's eyes were glowing with a golden light as he entered Fenneben's study, and the Dean noted the wonderful change from the big, awkward fellow with a bulldog countenance to this self-poised gentleman whose fine face it was a joy to see.

"I have a message for you, Burleigh. No hurry about it I was told, but I am called away on important business and I must get it out of my mind. An odd-looking fellow called at my door on the night I came home and left a package for you. He said he had tried to find you and failed, that he was a stranger here, and that you would understand the message inside. He insisted on not giving this in any hurry, and as my coming home has brought me a mass of things to consider, I have not been prompt about it."

Fenneben put a small package into Burleigh's hands.

"Examine it here, if you care to. You can fasten the door when you leave. Goodby!" and he was gone.

Victor sat down and opened the package. Inside was a quaint little silver pitcher, much ornamented, with the initial B embossed on the smooth side.

"The lost pitcher—stolen the day my mother died—and I was warned never to try to find who stole it." He turned to the light of the west window.

"It is the very thing I found in the cave that night. The man who took it may have been over there." He glanced out of the window and saw a thin twist of blue smoke rising above the ledges across the river.

"Who can have had it all this time, and why return it now?" he questioned. As he turned the pitcher in his hands a paper fell out.

"The message inside!" He spread out the paper and read "the message inside."

Well for him that Dr. Fenneben had left him alone. The shining face and eyes aglow changed suddenly to a white, hard countenance as he read this message inside. It ran:

"Victor Burleigh. First, don't ever try to follow me. The day you do I'll send you where I sent your father. No Burleigh can stay near me and live. Now be wise.

"Second. You saved the baby I left in the old dugout. Before God I never meant to kill it then. The thought of it has cursed my soul night and day till I found out you had saved him.

"Third. The girl you want to marry—go and marry. Do anything, good or bad, to destroy Burgess.

"Fourth. The money Burgess had is yours, only because I'm giving it to you. It belongs to Bug Buler. He couldn't talk plain when you saved him. He's not Bug Buler; he's Bug Burleigh, son of Victor Burleigh, heir to V. B.'s money in the law. I've got all the proofs. You see why you can have that money. Nobody will ever know but me. Don't hunt for me and I'll never tell. TOM GRESH."

The paper fell from Victor Burleigh's hands. The world, that ten minutes ago was a rose-hued sunset land, was a dreary midnight waste now. The one barrier between himself and Elinor had fallen only to rise up again.

Then came Satan into the game. "Nobody knew this but Gresh! Who had saved Bug's life? Who had cared for him and would always care for him? Why should Bug, little, loving Bug, come now to spoil his hopes? If Bug knew he would be first to give it all to his beloved Vic."

And then came Satan's ten strike. "No need to settle things now. Wait and think it over." And Vic decided in a blind way to think it over.

In the rotunda he met Trench, old Trench, slow of step but a lightning calculator.

"Where are you going?" he exclaimed, as he saw Vic's face.

"I'm going to the whirlpool before I'm through," Vic said, hoarsely.

Trench caught him in a powerful grip and shoved him to the foot of the rotunda stairs.

"No,-you re-not-going-to-the-whirlpool,"' he said, slowly. "You're going up to the top of the dome right against that *Ad Astra per Aspera* business up there, and open the west window and look out at the world the Lord made to heal hurt souls by looking at. And you are going to stay up there until you have fought the thing out with yourself, and come down like Moses did with the ten Commandments cut deep on the tables of your stony old heart. If you don't, you'll not need to go to old Lagonda's pool. By the holy saints, I'll take you there myself and plunge you in just to rid the world of such a fool. You hear me! Now, go on! And remember in your tussle that that big S cut over the old Sunrise door out there stands for Service. That's what will make your name fit you yet, Victor."

Vic slowly climbed up to where an hour ago the sudden opportunity for the fruition of his young life and hope had been brought to him. Lost now, unless—Nobody would ever know and Bug could lose nothing. He opened the west window and looked out at the Walnut Valley, dim and shadowy now, and the silver prairies beyond it and the gorgeous crimson tinted sky wherefrom the sun had slipped. And then and there, with his face to the light, he wrestled with the black Apollyon of his soul. And every minute the temptation grew to keep the funds "in trust," and to keep on caring for the boy he had cared for since babyhood. He clinched his white teeth and the tiger light was in his eyes again as the longing for Elinor's love overcame him. He pictured her as only one sunset ago she had looked up into his eyes, her face transfigured with love's sweetness, and he wished he might keep that picture forever. But, somehow, between that face and his own, came the picture of little Bug alone in the wretched dugout, reaching up baby arms to him for life and safety; on his baby face a pleading trustfulness.

Victor unbuttoned his cuff and slipped up his sleeve to the scar on his arm.

"Anybody can see the scar I put there when I cut out the poison," he said to himself, at last. "Nobody will see the scar on my soul, but I'll cut out the poison just the same. I did not save that baby boy from the rattlesnakes only to let him be crushed by the serpent in me. Trench was right, the S over the doorway down there stands for Service as well as for Sacrifice and Strife. Dr. Fenneben says they all enter into the winning of a Master's Degree. Shall I ever get mine earned, I wonder?"

He looked once more at the west, all a soft purple, gray-veiled with misty shadows, save over the place where the sun went out one shaft of deepest rose hue tipped with golden flame was cleaving its way toward the darkening zenith. Then he closed the window and went downstairs and out into the beautiful December twilight.

In all Kansas in that evening hour no man breathed deeper of the sweet, pure air, nor walked with firmer stride, than the man who had gone out under the carved symbol of the college doorway, Victor Burleigh of the junior class at Sunrise.

SUPREMACY

Make thyself free of Manhood's guild,
Pull down thy barns and greater build,
Pluck from the sunset's fruit of gold,
Glean from the heavens and ocean old,
From fireside lone and trampling street
Let thy life garner daily wheat,
The epic of a man rehearse,
Be something better than thy verse,
And thou shalt hear the life-blood flow
From farthest stars to grass-blades low.
—LOWELL

## CHAPTER XIII. THE MAN BELOW THE SMOKE

*And forgive us our debts as we forgive our debtors.*

ELINOR WREAM was standing at the gate as Victor Burleigh came striding up the street.

"Where are you going so fast, Victor?" she asked. "Everybody is in a rush this evening. We had a telegram from the East this afternoon. Uncle Joshua is very ill, and Uncle Lloyd had to get away on short notice. Old Bond Saxon went by just now, but," lowering her voice, "he was awfully drunk and slipped along like a snake."

"Have you seen Bug?" Victor asked. "Dennie says he left a little while ago to find his ball he lost out north this afternoon. He wouldn't tell where, because he had promised not to."

"No, I have not seen him. But don't be uneasy about Bug. He never plays near the river, nor the railroad tracks, and he always comes in at the right time," Elinor said, comfortingly.

"I know he always has before, but I want to find him, anyhow." The affectionate tone told Elinor what a loving guardianship was given to the unknown orphan child.

"There was a man here to see Uncle Lloyd just after he left this evening. The same man that brought a little package for you the night we came home. I suppose he comes from your part of the state out West, for he seemed to know you and Bug. He asked me if Bug ever played along the river and if he was a shy child. He was a strange-looking man, and I thought he had the cruelest face I ever saw, but I am no expert on strange faces."

Victor did not wait for another word.

"I must find Bug right away. You can't think what he is to me, Elinor," and he hurried away.

At the bend in the Walnut Vic saw Bug's little scarlet stocking cap beside the flat stone. The twilight was almost gone, but the glistening river reflected on the torn bushes above the bank-full stream.

The crushing agony of the first minutes made them seem like hours. And then the college discipline put in its work. Vic stopped and reasoned.

"Bug isn't down there. He never goes near the river. That strange man is Tom Gresh. He killed my father and he's laid a trap for me. He doesn't want to kill Bug. He wants to keep him to workout vengeance and hate on me. He says he'll send me to my father if I go near him. Well, I'm going so near he'll not doubt who I am, and I'll have Bug unharmed if I have to send Gresh where my father could not go even with water to cool his tongue. A man may fight with a man as he would fight with a beast to save himself or something dearer than himself from beastly destruction, Fenneben says. That's the battle before me now, and it's to the death."

The tiger light was in the yellow eyes as never before and the stern jaw was set, as Victor Burleigh hurried away. And this was the man who, such a little while ago, was debating with himself over the quiet possession of Bug Buler's inheritance. Truly the Mastery comes very near to such as he.

It was with tiger-like step and instinct, too, that the young man went leaping up the dark, frost-coated glen. About the mouth of the cave the blackness was appalling. It seemed a place apart, cursed with the frown of Nature. Yet in the April time, the sweetest moments of Vic's young life had been spent in this very spot that now showed all the difference between Love and Hate.

As he neared the opening of the cavern he guarded his footsteps more carefully. The jungle beast was alert within him and the college training was giving way to the might of muscle backed by a will to win.

A dim light gleamed in the cave and he watched outside now, as Gresh on the April day had watched him inside. Down by a wood fire, whose smoke was twisting out through a crevice overhead somewhere, little Bug was sitting on Tom Gresh's big coat, the fire lighting up his tangle of red-brown curls. His big brown eyes looking up at the man crouching by the fire were eyes of innocent courage, and the expression on the sweet child-face was impenetrable.

"He's a Burleigh. He's not afraid," Vic thought, exultingly. "That's half my battle. I had it out with the rattlesnakes. I'll do better here."

At that moment the outlaw turned toward the door and leaped to his feet as Vic sprang inside.

Bug started up with outstretched arms.

"Keep out of the way, Bug," Vic cried, as the two men clinched.

And the struggle began. They were evenly matched, and both had the sinews of giants. The outlaw had the advantage of an iron strength, hardened by years of out-door life. But the college that had softened the country boy somewhat gave in return the quick judgment and superior agility of the trained power that counts against weight before the battle is over. But withal, it was terrible. One fighter was a murderer by trade, his hand steady for the blackest deeds, and here was a man he had waited long months to destroy. The other fighter was in the struggle to save a life dear to him, a life that must vindicate his conscience and preserve his soul's peace.

Across the stone-floored cave they threshed in fury, until at the farther wall Gresh flung Vic from him against the jagged rock with a force that cut a gash across the boy's head. The blood splashed on both men's faces as they renewed the strife. Then with a quick twist Burleigh threw the outlaw to the floor and held him in a clutch that weighed him down like a ledge of rock; and it was pound for pound again.

Away from the mass of burning coals the blackness was horrible. Beyond that fire Bug sat, silent as the stone wall behind him. Gresh gained the mastery again, and with a grip on Vic's throat was about to thrust his head, face downward, into the burning embers. Vic understood and strove for his own life with a maniac's might, for he knew that one more wrench would end the thing.

"You first, and then the baby; I'll roast you both," Gresh hissed, and Vic smelled the heat of the wood flame.

But who had counted on Bug? He had watched this fearful grapple, motionless and terror-stricken, and now with a child's vision he saw what Gresh meant to do. Springing up, he caught the heavy coat on which he had been sitting and flung it on the fire, smothering the embers and putting the cavern into complete darkness.

Vic gained the vantage by this unlooked for movement and the grip shifted. The fighters fell to the floor and then began the same kind of struggle by which Burleigh had out-generaled big, unconquerable Trench one day. The two had rolled and fought in college combat from the top of the limestone ridge to the lower campus and landed with Burleigh gripping Trench helpless to defend further. That battle was friend with friend. This battle was to the death. The blood of both men smeared the floor as they tore at each other like wild beasts, and no man could have told which oftenest had the vantage hold, nor how the strife would end. But it did end soon. The heavy coat, that had smothered the fire and saved Vic, smoldered a little, then flared into flame, lighting the whole cave, and throwing out black and awful shadows of the two fighters. They were close to the hole in the inner wall now. Gresh's face in that unsteady glare was horrible to see. He loosed his hold a second, then lunged at Vic with the fury of a mad brute. And Vic, who had fought the devil in himself to a standstill three hours ago, now caught the fiend outside of him for a finishing blow, and the strength of that last struggle was terrific.

Up to this time Vic had not spoken.

"I killed the other snakes. I'll kill you now," he growled, as he held the outlaw at length in a conquering grip, his knees on Gresh's breast, his right hand on Gresh's throat.

In that weird light the conqueror's face was only a degree less brutal than the outlaw's face. And Burleigh meant every word, for murder was in his heart and in his clutching fingers. Beneath the weight of his strength Gresh slowly relaxed, struggling fiercely at first and groping blindly to escape. Then he began to whine for mercy, but his whining maddened his conqueror more than his blows had done. For such strife is no mere wrestling match. Every blow struck against a fellowman is as the smell of blood to the tiger, feeding a fiendish eagerness to kill. Beside, Burleigh had ample cause for vengeance. The creature under his grip was not only a bootlegger through whose evil influence men took other lives or lost their own; he had slain one innocent man, Vic's own father, and in the room where his dead mother lay had robbed Vic's home of every valuable thing. He had sworn vengeance on all who bore the name of Burleigh. What fate might await Bug, Vic dared not picture. One strangling grip now could finish the business forever, and his clutch tightened, as Gresh lay begging like a coward for his own worthless life.

"It's a good thing a fellow has a guardian angel once in a while. We get pretty close to the edge sometimes and never know how near we are to destruction," Vic had said to Elinor in here on the April day.

It was not Vic's guardian angel, but little Bug whose white face was thrust between him and his victim, and the touch of a soft little hand and the pleading child-voice that cried:

"Don't kill him, Vic. He's frough of fighting now. Don't hurt him no more."

Vic staid his hand at the words. The few minutes of this mad-beast duel had made him forget the sound of human voices. He half lifted himself from Gresh's body at Bug's cry. And Bug, wise beyond his years, quaint-minded little Bug, said, softly:

"Fordive us our debts as we fordive our debtors."

Strange, loving words of the Man of Galilee, spoken on the mountain-side long, long ago, and echoed now by childish lips in the dying light of the cavern to these two men, drunk with brute-lust for human blood! For Vic the words struck like blows. All the years since his father's death he had waited for this hour. At last he had met and vanquished the man who had taken his father's life, and now, exultant in his victory, came this little child's voice.

The cave darkened. A mist, half blood, half blindness, came before his eyes, but clear to his ears there sounded the ringing words:

"Vengeance is mine; I will repay!"

It was the voice of Discipline calling to his better judgment, as Bug's innocent pleading spoke to the finer man within him.

Under his grip Gresh lay motionless, all power of resistance threshed out of him.

"Are you ready to quit?" Vic questioned, hoarsely, bending over the almost lifeless form.

The outlaw mumbled assent.

"Then I'll let you live, you miserable wretch, and the courts will take care of you."

Burleigh himself was faint from strife and loss of blood. As he relaxed his vigilance the last atom of strength, the last hope of escape returned to Gresh. He sprang to his feet, staggered blindly then, quick as a panther, he leaped through the hole in the farther wall, wriggled swiftly into the blind crevices of the inner cave, and was gone.

It was Trench who dressed Vic's head that night and shielded him until his strength returned. But it was Bond Saxon who counseled patience.

"Don't squeal to the sheriff now," he urged. "The scoundrel is gone, and it would make a nine days' hooray, and nothing would come of it. He was darned slick to take the time when Funnybone was away."

"Why?" Vic asked.

But Bond would not tell why. And Vic never dreamed how much cause Bond Saxon had to dread the day when Tom Gresh should be brought into court, and his own great crime committed in his drunken hours would demand retribution. So Lagonda Ledge and Sunrise knew nothing of what had occurred. Burleigh had no recourse but to wait, while Bug buttoned up his lips, as he had done for Burgess out at Pigeon Place, and conveniently "fordot" what he chose not to tell. But he wandered no more alone about the pretty by-corners of Lagonda Ledge.

## CHAPTER XIV. THE DERELICTS

I dimly guess from blessings known
   Of greater out of sight,
And, with the chastened Psalmist, own
   His judgments, too, are right.

I know not what the future hath
   Of marvel or surprise,
Assured alone that life and death
   His mercy underlies.
                    —WHITTIER

IT was early spring before Dr. Fenneben returned to Lagonda Ledge. Everybody thought the new line on his face was put there by the death of his brother. To those who loved him most—that is, to all Lagonda Ledge—he was growing handsomer every year, and even with this new expression his countenance wore a more kindly grace than ever before.

"Norrie, your uncle was a strange man," Fenneben declared, as he and Elinor sat in the library on the evening of his return. "Naturally, I am unlike my stepbrothers, but I have not even understood them. There were many things I learned at Joshua's bedside that I never knew of the family before. There were some things for you to know, but not now."

"I can trust you, Uncle Lloyd, to do just the right thing," Norrie declared.

The new line of sadness deepened in Lloyd Fenneben's face.

"That is a hard thing to do sometimes. Your trust will help me wonderfully, however," he replied. "My brother in his last hours made urgent requests of me and pled with me until I pledged my word to carry out his wishes. Here's where I need your trust most."

Elinor bent over her uncle and softly stroked the heavy black hair from his forehead.

"Here's where I help you most, then," she said, gently.

"I have some funds, Elinor, to be yours at your graduation—not before. Believe me, dear girl, I begged of Joshua to let me turn them over to you now, but he staid obstinate to the last."

"And I don't want a thing different till I get my diploma. Not even till I get my Master's Degree for that matter," Elinor said, playfully.

"And meantime, Norrie, will you just be a college girl and drop all thought of this marrying business until you are through school?" Fenneben was hesitating a little now. "A year hence will be time enough for that."

"Most gladly," Elinor assured him.

"Then that's all for my brother's sake. Now for mine, Norrie, or for yours, rather, if my little girl has her mind all set about things after school days, I hope she will not be a flirt. Sometimes the words and acts cut deeper into other lives than we ever dream. Norrie, I know this out of the years of my own lonely life."

Elinor's eyes were dewy with tears and she bent her head until her hair touched his cheek.

"I'll try to be good 'fornever,' as Bug Buler says," she murmured.

Over in the Saxon House on this same evening Vincent Burgess had come in to see Dennie about some books.

"I took your advice, Dennie," he said. "I have been a man to the extent of making myself square with Victor Burleigh, and I've felt like a free man ever since."

The look of joy and pride in Dennie's eyes thrilled him with a keen pleasure. Her eyes were of such a soft gray and her pretty wavy hair was so lustrous tonight.

"Dennie, I am going to be even more of a man than you asked me to be."

Dennie did not look up. The pink of her cheek, her long lashes over her downcast eyes, the sunny curls above her forehead, all were fair to Vincent Burgess. As he looked at her he began to understand, blind bat that he had been all this time, he, Professor Vincent Burgess, A.B., Instructor in Greek from Harvard University.

"I must be going now. Good-night, Dennie."

He shook hands and hurried away, but to the girl who was earning her college education there was something in his handclasp, denied before.

The next day there was a settling of affairs at Sunrise, and the character-building put into Lloyd Fenneben's hand, as clay for the potter's wheel, seemed to him to be shaping somewhat to its destined uses.

Again, Vincent Burgess sat in the chair by the west study window, acting-dean, now seeking neither types, nor geographical breadth, nor seclusion amid barren prairie lands for profound research in preparing for a Master's Degree.

With no effort to conceal matters, except the fact that the trust funds had first belonged to his own sister and brother-in-law, he explained to Fenneben the line of events connecting him with Victor Burleigh.

"And, Dr. Fenneben, I must speak of a matter I have never touched upon with you before. It was agreed between Dr. Wream and myself that I should become his nephew by marriage. I want to go to Miss Elinor and ask her to release me. You will pardon my frankness, for I cannot honorably continue in this relationship since I have restored the property to Victor Burleigh."

"He thinks she will not care for him now," Fenneben said to himself. Aloud he said:

"Have you ever spoken directly to Elinor on this matter?"

"N-no. It was an understanding between her and her uncle and between him and me," Burgess replied.

"Well, I don't pretend to know girls very well, being a confirmed bachelor"—the Dean's eyes were smiling—"but my advice at this distance is not to ask Norrie to release you from what she herself has never yet bound you. I'll vouch for her peace of mind; and your sense of honor is fully vindicated now. To be equally frank with you, Burgess, now that Norrie is entirely in my charge, I have put this sort of thing for her absolutely into the after-commencement years. The best wife is not always the girl who wears a diamond ring through three or four years of her college life. I want my niece to be a girl now, not a bride-in-waiting."

As Burgess rose to go his eye caught sight of the pigeons above the bend in the river.

"By the way, Doctor, have you ever found out anything about the woman who used to live in that deserted place up north?"

"Nothing yet," Fenneben replied. "But, remember, I have not spent a week—that is, a sane week—in Lagonda Ledge since the night you, and she, and Saxon, and the dog saved my life. I shall take up her case soon."

"She is gone away and nobody knows where, Saxon tells me," Burgess said. "For many reasons I wish we could find her, but she has dropped out of sight."

Lloyd Fenneben wondered at the sorrowful expression on the younger man's face when he said this.

As he left the study Victor Burleigh came in.

"Sit down, Burleigh. What can I do for you?" Fenneben asked.

Something like his own magnetism of presence was in the young man before him.

"I want to tell you something," Vic responded.

"Let me tell you something. I knew you had good blood in your veins even when I saw you kill that bull snake. Burgess has just been in. He has told me his side of your story. Noble fellow he is to free himself of a life-long slavery to somebody else's dollars. However

147

much a man may try to hide the fetters of unlawful gains, they clank in his own ears till he hates himself. Now Burgess is a freeman."

"I am glad to hear you say so, Dr. Fenneben. It makes my own freedom sweeter," Vic declared.

"Yes," Fenneben replied. "Your added means will bring you life's best gift—opportunity."

"I have no added means, Doctor. I have funds in trust for Bug Buler, and I come to ask you to take his legal guardianship for me." And then he told his own life story.

"So the heroism shifts to you as well. I can picture the cost to a man like yourself," the Dean said. "Have you no record of Bug's father and mother?"

"None but the record given by Dr. Wream. They are dead," Burleigh replied. "His father may have met the same fate that my father did."

"Why don't you take the guardianship yourself, Burleigh? The boy is yours in love and blood. He ought to be in law."

Victor Burleigh stood up to his full height, a magnificent product of Nature's handiwork. But the mind and soul "Dean Funnybone" had helped to shape.

"I will be honest with you, Dr. Fenneben," Burleigh said, and his voice was deep and sweetly resonant. "If I keep the money in charge I may not be proof against the temptation to use it for myself. As strong as my strong arms are my hates and loves, and for some reasons I would do almost anything to gain riches. I might not resist the tempter."

Lloyd Fenneben's black eyes blazed at the words.

"I understand perfectly what you mean, but no woman who exacts this price is worth the cost." Then, in a gentler tone, he continued: "Burleigh, will you take my advice? I have always had your welfare on my heart. Finish your college work first. Get the best of the classroom, the library, the athletic field, and the 'picnic spread.' Is that the right term? But fit yourself for manhood before you undertake a man's duties. Meantime, He who has given you the mastery in the years behind you is leading you toward the larger places before you, teaching you all the meanings of Strife, and Sacrifice, and Service symbolized above our doorway in our proud College initial letter. The Supremacy is yet to come. Will you follow my counsel? I'll take care of Bug, and we will keep Burgess out of this for a while."

Burleigh thought he understood, and the silent hand clasp pledged the faith of the country boy to the teacher's wishes.

It is only in story books that events leap out as pages are turned, events that take days on days of real life to compass. In the swing of one brief year Lagonda Ledge knew little change. New cement walks were built south almost to the Kickapoo Corral. A new manufacturing concern had bonds voted for it at an exciting election, and a squabble for a suitable site was in process. Vincent Burgess and Victor Burleigh, two strong men, were growing actually chummy, and Trench declared he was glad they had decided to quit playing marbles for keeps and hiding each other's caps.

And now the springtime of the year was on the beautiful Walnut Valley. Elinor and Dennie, Trench, "Limpy," the crippled student, and Victor Burleigh were all on the home-stretch of their senior year. One more June Commencement day and Sunrise would know them no more. Beyond all this there was nothing new at Lagonda Ledge until suddenly the white-haired woman was up at Pigeon Place, again, a fact known only to old Bond Saxon and little Bug, who saw her leave the train. The little blue smoke-twist was again rising lazily in the warm May air, and somebody was systematically robbing houses in town, and Bond Saxon was often drunk and hiding away from sight. A May storm sent the Walnut booming down the valley, bank full, cutting off traffic at the town bridge, but the days that followed were a joy. A tenderly green world it was now, all blossom-decked, and blown across by the gentle May zephyrs, with nothing harsh nor cruel in it, unless the rushing river down below the shallows might seem so. The Kickapoo Corral, luxuriant with flowers, and springing grass, and May green foliage, told nothing of the old-time siege and sorrow of Swift Elk and the Fawn of the Morning Light.

On the night after the storm Professor Burgess stopped at the Saxon House.

"Where is your father, Dennie?" he asked.

"He went up north to help somebody out of the mud and water, I suppose," Dennie replied. "He is the kindest neighbor, and he has been trying to—to keep straight. He told me when he left that this night's work was to be a work of redemption for him. He may get stronger some time."

In his heart Burgess knew better. He had no faith in the old man's will power, and the burden of a hidden crime he knew would but increase its weight with time, and drag Bond down at last. But Dennie need not suffer now.

"Will you go with me down to the old Corral tomorrow afternoon, Dennie? I want some plants that grow there. I'm studying nature along with Greek," he said, smiling.

"Of course, if it is fair," Dennie replied, the pretty color blooming deeper in her cheeks.

"Oh, we go fair or foul. You remember we fought it out coming home from there once."

Meanwhile Bond Saxon was hurrying north on his work of redemption. At the bend in the river he found Tom Gresh sitting on the flat stone slab. The light was gleaming through the shrubbery of the little cottage, and the homey sounds of evening and the twitter of late-coming birds were in the air.

"What are you here for, Gresh?" Bond asked, hoarsely. "I thought you had left for good."

The villainous-looking outlaw drew a flask from his pocket.

"Have a drink, Saxon. Take the whole bottle," and he thrust it into the old man's hands.

Bond wavered a moment, then flung it far into the foamy floods of the Walnut.

"Not any more. You shall not get me drunk again while you rob and kill."

"You did the killing for me once. Won't you do it again?" Gresh snarled.

Bond clinched his fists but did not strike.

"What are you after now?" he asked. "You are through with the Burleighs; Vic settled you and you know it."

Even with the words the clutch of Vic's fingers on the outlaw's throat seemed to choke him now.

"If my last Burleigh is gone," he growled with an oath, "I'm not done yet. There's Elinor Wream. Don't forget that her mother was my adopted sister. Don't forget that my old foster father cut me off without a cent and gave her all his money. That's why Nathan Wream married her. He wanted her money for colleges." The sneer on the man's face was diabolical. "I can hit the old man through Elinor, and I'll do it some time, and that's not the only blow that I can strike here, and I am going to finish this thing now." He pointed toward the cottage where the unprotected woman sat alone. "Twice I've nerved myself to do it and been fooled each time. One October day you were here drunk. I could have laid it on you easy, and maybe fixed Fenneben too, if a little child's voice hadn't scared me stiff. And the day of the big football game you wouldn't get drunk and she must go down to that game just to look once at Lloyd Fenneben. I meant to finish her that day. This is the third and last time now. There is not even a dog to protect her."

Bond Saxon had been a huge fellow in his best days, and now he summoned all the powers nature had left to him.

"Tom Gresh," he cried, "in my infernal weakness you made me a drunken beast, who took the life of an innocent man you wanted out of your way. You thought, you fool, that she might care for you then. I've carried the curse of that deed on my soul night and day. I'll wipe it partly away now by saving her life from you. So surely as tonight, tomorrow, or ever you try to harm her, I'll not show you the mercy Vic Burleigh showed you once."

Strange forms the guardian angel takes!

Hence we entertain it unawares.

Of all Lagonda Ledge, old Bond Saxon, standing between a woman and the peril of her life, looked least angelic. Gresh understood him and turned first in fawning and tempting trickery to his adversary. But Saxon stood his ground. Then the outlaw raged in fury, not daring to strike now, because he knew Bond's strength. And still the old man was unmoved. A life saved for the life he had taken was steeling his soul to courage.

At last in the dim light, Gresh stood motionless a minute, then he struck his parting blow.

"All right, Bond Saxon, play protector all you want to, but it's a short game for you. The sheriff is out of town tonight, but tomorrow afternoon he will get back to Lagonda Ledge. Tomorrow afternoon I go with all my proofs—Oh, I've got 'em. And you, Bond Saxon, will be behind the bars for your crime, done not so many years ago, and your honorable daughter, disgraced forever by you, can shift for herself. I've nothing to lose; why should I protect you?"

He leaped down the bank into the swiftly flowing river, and, swimming easily to the farther side, he disappeared in the underbrush.

The next afternoon, somebody remembered that Bond Saxon had crossed the bridge and plunged into the overflow of the river around the west end. But Bond had been drunk much of late and nobody approached him when he was drunk. How could Lagonda Ledge know the agony of the old man's soul as he splashed across the Walnut waters and floundered up the narrow glen to the cave? Or how, for Dennie's sake, he had begged on his knees for mercy that should save his daughter's name? Or how harder than the stone of the ledges, that the trickling water through slow-dragging centuries has worn away, was the stony heart of the creature who denied him?

And only Victor Burleigh had power to picture the struggle that must have followed in that cavern, and beyond the wall into the blind black passages leading at last to the bluff above the river, where, clinched in deadly combat, the two men, fighting still, fell headlong into the Walnut floods.

Down at the shallows Professor Burgess and Dennie had found the waters too deep to reach the Kickapoo Corral, so they strolled along the bluff watching the river rippling merrily in the fall of the afternoon sunshine. And brightly, too, the sunshine fell on Dennie Saxon's rippling hair, recalling to Vincent Burgess' memory the woodland camp fire and the old legend told in the October twilight and the flickering flames lighting Dennie's face and the wavy folds of her sunny hair.

But even as he remembered, a cry up stream came faintly, once and no more, while, grappling still, two forms were borne down by the swift current to the bend above the whirlpool. Dennie and Vincent sprang to the very edge of the bluff, powerless to save, as Tom Gresh and Bond Saxon were swept around the curve below the Corral. Across the shallows they struggled for a footing, but the undertow carried them on toward the fatal pool.

A shriek from the bank came to Bond Saxon's ears, and he looked up and saw the two reaching out vain hands to him.

"Your oath, Vincent; your oath!" he cried in agonizing tones.

Then Vincent Burgess put one arm about Dennie Saxon and drew her close to him and lifted up his right hand high above him in token to the drowning man of his promise, under heaven, to keep that oath forever.

A look of joy swept over the old face in the water, his struggling ceased, and once more tribute was paid to the grim Chieftain of Lagonda's Pool. — — — —

They said about town the next day that it was the peacefulest face ever seen below a coffin lid. And, remembering only his many acts of neighborly kindness, they forgave and forgot his weaknesses, while to the few who knew his life-tragedy came the assuring hope that the forgiving mercy of man is but a type of the boundless mercy of a forgiving God.

## CHAPTER XV. THE MASTERY

And only the Master shall praise us, and only the Master shall
blame,
And no one shall work for money, and no one shall work for
fame,
But each for the joy of working, and each, in his  separate star,
Shall draw the Thing as he sees It for the God of Things as They
Are.
    —KIPLING

JUNE time in the Walnut Valley, and commencement time at Sunrise
on the limestone ridge! Nor pen nor brush can show the glory of the
radiant prairies, and the deep blue of the "unscarred heavens," and
the bright gleams from rippling waters. And at the end of a perfect
day comes the silvery grandeur of a moonlit June night.

It was late afternoon of the day before commencement. Victor
Burleigh stood on the stone where four years ago the bull snake had
stretched itself in the lazy sunshine. Only one more day at Sunrise
for him, and the little heartache, unlike any other sorrow a life can
ever know, was his, as he stood there. In the four years' battle he had
come off conqueror until the symbol above the doorway no longer
held any mystery for him. His character and culture now matched
his voice. Before him was higher learning, an under-professorship at
Harvard, and later on the pulpit for his life work. But now the
heartache of parting was his, and a deeper pain than breaking school
ties was his also. A year of jolly goodfellowship was ending, a happy
year, with Elinor his most frequent companion. And often in this
year he had wondered at Lloyd Fenneben's harsh judgment of her.
Fondness of luxury seemed foreign to her, and womanly beauty of
character made her always "Norrie the beloved." But Victor was true
to Fenneben's demands and willing to try to live through the years
after, if one year of happy association could be his now. Whatever
claims Burgess might assert later, he could not take from another the
claim to happy memories. But, today, there was the dull steady
heartache that he knew had come to stay.

Presently Elinor joined him.

"May I come down tonight for a goodby stroll, Elinor? There's a full moon and after tomorrow there are to be no more moons, nor stars, nor suns, nor lands, nor seas, nor principalities, nor powers for us at Sunrise."

"I wish you would come, Victor," Elinor said. "Come early. There's a crowd going out somewhere, and we can join the ranks of the great ungraduated for the last time."

"Elinor, I'm not hunting a crowd tonight," Vic said in a low voice.

"Well, come, anyway, and we'll hunt the solitude, if we can't hunt any other game." And they strolled homeward together.

In the early evening Lloyd Fenneben and Elinor sat on the veranda watching the sunset through the trees beyond the river.

"You are to graduate from Sunrise tomorrow," Dr. Fenneben was saying. "For a Wream that is the real beginning of life. I have your business matters entrusted to me, ready to close up as soon as you are 'legally graduated' according to my brother's wishes, but you may as well know them now."

He paused, and Elinor, thinking of the moonlight, maybe, waited in peaceful silence.

"Norrie, when I finished at the university my brother put a small fortune into my hands and bade me go West and build a new Harvard. You know our family hold that that is the only legitimate use for money."

Norrie smiled assent.

"I did not ask whose money it was, for my brother handled many bequests, and I was a poor business man then. I came and invested it at last in Sunrise-by-the-Walnut. That was your mother's money, given by your father to Joshua, who gave it to me. Joshua did not tell me, and I supposed some good, old Boston philanthropist had bought an indulgence for his ignorant soul by endowing this thing so freely. I found it out on Joshua's deathbed, and only to pacify him would I consent to keep it until now. Henceforth, it must be yours. That is why I asked you a year ago to just be a college girl and drop all thought about marrying. I wanted you to come into possession of your own property before you bound yourself by any bonds you could not break."

Elinor sat silent for a while, her dark eyes seeing only the low golden sunset. She understood now what had grooved that line of care in Lloyd Fenneben's face when he came home from the East. But he had conquered, aye, he had won the mastery.

"And you and Sunrise?" she asked at length.

"I can sell the college site and buildings to this new manufactory coming here in August. Added to this, I have acquired sufficient funds of my own to pay you the entire amount and a good rate of interest with it. My grief is that for all these years, I have kept you out of your own."

Elinor rose up, white and cold, and put her hand on her uncle's hand.

"Let me think a little, Uncle Lloyd. It is not easy to realize one's fortune in a minute." Then she left him.

"It makes little difference what passion possesses a man's soul, if it possesses him he will wrong his fellowmen," Fenneben said to himself. "In Joshua Wream's craving to endow college claims he robbed this girl of her inheritance and sent her to me, telling me she was shallow-minded and wholly given to a love of luxuries, that I might not see his plans; while Norrie, never knowing, has proved over and over how false these charges were. And at last, to still his noisy conscience, he would marry her, willing or unwilling, to Vincent Burgess. But with all this, his last hours were full of sorrowful confession. What do these Masters' Degrees my brother bore avail a man if he have not the mastery within? Meanwhile, my labors here must end."

Lonely and crushed, with his life work taken from him, he sat and faced the sunset. Presently, he saw Elinor and Victor Burleigh strolling away in the soft evening light. At the corner, Elinor turned and waved a good-by to him. Then the memory of his own commencement day came back to him, and of the happy night before. Oh, that night before! Can a man ever forget! And now, tonight!

"Don Fonnybone," Bug Buler piped, as he came trudging around the corner. "I want to confessing."

He came to Fenneben's side and looked up confidently in his face.

"Well, confessing. I've just finished doing that myself," Fenneben said.

"I did a bad, long ago. I want to go and confessing. Will you go with me?"

"Where shall we go to be shriven, Bug?

"To Pigeon Place," Bug responded. "The Pigeon woman is there now. I saw her coming, and I must go right away and confessing."

"I'll go with you, Bug. I want to see that woman, anyhow," Fenneben said.

And the two went away in the early twilight of this rare June evening.

Out at Pigeon Place, when Dr. Fenneben and little Bug walked up the grassy way to the vine-covered porch in the misty twilight, Mrs. Marian sat in the shadow, unaware of their coming until they stood before her.

Lloyd Fenneben lifted his hat, and little Bug imitated him.

"I beg your pardon, Mrs. Marian. This little boy wanted to tell you of something that was troubling him. I think he trespassed on your property unknowingly."

The gray-haired woman stood motionless in the shadow still. Her fair face less haggard than of yore, as if some dread had left it, and only loneliness remained.

"I was here, and you was away, and I peeked in the window. It was rude and I never did see you to tell you, and I'm sorry and I won't for—never do it again. Dennie told me to come tonight, and bring Don Fonnybone." Bug had his part well in hand.

Even as she smiled at him, Dr. Fenneben noticed how her hand on the lattice shook.

"And I want to thank you, Mrs. Marian, for your bravery and goodness on the night I was assaulted here." Fenneben was a gentleman to the core and his courtesy was charming. "I meant to find you long ago, but my brother's death, with my own long illness, and your absence, and my many duties—" He paused with a smile.

"Oh, Lloyd, Lloyd, on an evening like this, why do you come here?"

The woman stood in the light now, a tragic figure of sorrow. And she was not yet forty.

Dr. Fenneben caught his breath and the light seemed to go out before him.

"Marian, oh, Marian! After all these years, do I find you here? They said you were dead." He caught her in his arms and held her close to his breast.

"Lots of folks spoons round the Saxon House, so I went away and lef 'em," Bug explained to Vic once afterward.

And that accounted for little Bug sitting lonely on the flat stone by the bend in the river where Dennie and Burgess found him later.

"So you have stood between me and that assassin all these years, even when the lies against me made you doubt my love. Oh, Marian, the strength of a woman's heart!" Fenneben declared, as, side by side, black hair and the gray near together, these long-separated lovers rebuilt their world.

"And this little child brought you here at last. 'A little child shall lead them,'" the woman murmured.

"Yes, Bug is a gift of God." Lloyd Fenneben was bending over her. "He is Victor Burleigh's nephew, who found him in a deserted place—"

A shriek cut the evening air and she who had been known as Mrs. Marian lay in a faint at Fenneben's feet.

"Tell me, Marian, what this means."

Lloyd Fenneben had restored her to consciousness and she was resting, white and trembling, in his arms.

"My little Bug, my baby, Burgess!" she sobbed. "Bond Saxon, in a drunken fit, killed his father. Then Tom Gresh carried him away to save him from Bond, too, so Tom declared, but I did not believe him. Bond never harmed a little child. Tom said he meant no harm and that Bug was stolen from where he had left him. It was then that my hair turned white. Tom tried once, a year ago in December, to make me believe he could bring Bug back to me if I would care for him— for that wicked murderer! Oh, Lloyd!"

She nestled close in Dr. Fenneben's protecting arms, and shivered at the thought.

"And you named him Burgess for your own name. Does Vincent know?" Fenneben questioned, tenderly smoothing the white hair as Norrie had so often smoothed his own.

"Is this Vincent my own brother? Will he really own me as his sister? I've tried to meet him many times. I left his picture on my table that he might see it if he should ever come. My father separated us years ago. After we came West he sent me just one letter in which he said Vincent would never speak to me nor claim me as his sister again. A brother—a lover—and my baby boy!"

And the lonely woman, overcome with joy, sat white and still beneath the white moonbeams.

Joy does not kill any more than sorrow. Vincent Burgess and Dennie Saxon, who came just at the right time, told how they had waited with Bug at the slab of stone by the bend in the river until they should be needed.

"It was Dennie who planned it all," Vincent said, "and did not even let me know. Bug told her my picture was on the table in there. But so long as her father lived, she kept her counsel."

"I tried four years ago to get Dr. Fenneben to come out here," Dennie said. And the Dean remembered the autumn holiday and Dennie's solicitude for an unknown woman.

But the joy of this night, crowning all other joys in the Walnut Valley, was in that sacred moment when Bug Buler walked slowly up to Marian Burleigh, sister to Vincent Burgess, lost love of Lloyd Fenneben's youth—slowly, and with big brown eyes glowing with a strange new love light, and, putting up both his chubby hands to her cheeks, he murmured softly:

"Is you my own mother? Then, I'll love you fornever."

Meantime, on this last moonlit June night, Elinor and Vic were strolling down the new south cement walk, a favorite place for the young people now.

At the farther end, Vic said:

"Norrie, let's go down across the shallows to the west bluff again. Can you climb it, or shall we join the crowd down in the Kickapoo Corral?"

"I can climb where you can, Victor," Elinor declared.

"Dennie will never want to come here again. Poor Dennie!"

Vic was helping Elinor across the shallows as he spoke. Up in the Corral a happy crowd of young people were finishing their last "picnic spread" for the year. Below the shallows the whirlpool was glistening all treacherously smooth and level under the moonbeams.

"Why 'poor Dennie,' Victor? Her father had nothing more for him, here, except disgrace. The tribute paid him at his funeral would have been forever withheld, if he had lived a day longer, and he died sure of Dennie's future." Elinor spoke gently.

"Who told you all this, Elinor?" Victor asked.

"Professor Burgess, when he showed me the diamond ring Dennie is to wear tomorrow."

"Dennie, a diamond! I'm glad for Dennie. Diamonds are fine to have," Vic declared.

They had climbed to the top of the west bluff. The silvery prairie and silver river and mist-wreathed valley, and overhead, the clear, calm sky, where the moon sailed in magnificent grandeur, were a setting to make the evening a perfect one. And in this setting was Elinor, herself the jewel, beautiful, winsome, womanly.

"I have some good news." She turned to the young man beside her. "You know the Wreams have made a life business of endowing colleges. Well, I am a Wream by blood, and tomorrow, oh, Victor, tomorrow, I, too, have the opportunity of a lifetime. I'm going to endow Sunrise."

He looked at her in amazement.

"Oh, it's clear enough," she exclaimed. "It was my money that built Sunrise. It shall stay here, and Dr. Lloyd Fenneben, Dean of Sunrise, and acting-Dean Vincent Burgess, A.B., Professor of Greek, and Victor Burleigh, Valedictorian, who goes East to a professorship in Harvard, and to the ministry of the gospel later on—all you mighty men of valor will know how little Norrie Wream cares for money, except as it can make the world better and happier. I haven't lived in Lloyd Fenneben's home these four years without learning something of what is required for a Master's Degree."

"Norrie!" All the music of a soul poured into the music of the deep voice.

"Victor! There is no sacrifice in it. I wish there were, that I might wear the honors you wear so modestly."

"I, Elinor?"

"I know the whole story. Dennie told me when you had that awful fight, and Trenchie told me long ago, that you thought I must have money to make me happy. Why I, more than Dennie, or you, who gave Bug his claim?"

Elinor put up her hands to Victor, who took them both in his, as he drew her to him and kissed her sweet red lips. And there was a new heaven and a new earth created that night in the soft silvery moonlight of the Walnut Valley.

"I'd rather be here with you than over the river with anybody else. I feel safer here," she murmured, remembering when they had striven in the darkness and the storm to reach this very height.

But Victor Burleigh could not speak. The mastery for which he had striven seemed to bring meed of reward too great for him to grasp with words.

## THE PARTING

... There is neither East nor West, Border,
    nor Breed, nor Birth,
When two strong men stand face to face, tho' they
    come from the ends of the earth!
        —KIPLING

COMMENCEMENT day at Sunrise was just one golden Kansas June day, when

The heart is so full that a drop overfills it.

Victor Burleigh, late of a claim out beyond the Walnut, Professor-to-be in Harvard University, and Vincent Burgess, acting-Dean of Sunrise, only a degree less beloved than Dean Fenneben himself, met on the morning of commencement day at the campus gate, one to go to the East, the other to stay in the West. Side by side they walked up the long avenue to the foot of the slope, together they climbed the broad flight of steps leading up to the imposing doorway of Sunrise with the big letter S carved in relief above it. And after pausing a moment to take in the matchless wonder of the landscape over which old Sunrise keeps watch, the college portal swung open and the two entered at the same time. Inside the doorway, under the halo of light from the stained glass dome with its Kansas motto, wrought in dainty coloring. Elinor Wream, niece of the Dean of Sunrise, and Dennie Saxon, old Bond Saxon's daughter, who had earned her college tuition, stood side by side, awaiting them. And beyond these, on the rotunda stairs, Dr. Lloyd Fenneben was looking down at the four with keen black eyes. Beside him on the broad stairway was Marian Burgess Burleigh, the white-haired, young-faced woman of Pigeon Place, and Bug Buler—everybody's child.

The barriers were down at last: the value of common life, the power of Strife and Sacrifice and Service, the joy of Supremacy, the conflict of rich red blood with the thinner blue, the force of culture against mere physical strength, the power of character over wealth—these things had been wrought out under the gracious influence of Dr. Lloyd Fenneben in Sunrise-by-the-Walnut.

"Come up, come up; there is room up here," the Dean called to the group in the rotunda. "There's an A.B. for all who have conquered the Course of Study, and a Master's Degree for everyone who has conquered himself."

The common level so impossible on a September day four years ago, came now to two strong men when the commencement exercises were ended, and Sunrise became to the outgoing class only a hallowed memory.

The hour is high noon, the good-bys are given, and from the crest of the limestone ridge the ringing chorus, led by good old Trench, sounds far and far away along the Walnut Valley:

Rah for Funnybone!
Rah for Funnybone!
Rah for Funnybone!
Rah! RAW RAH!!!

9 781034 813040